Lost Highway

Books by Richard Currey

FATAL LIGHT

THE WARS OF HEAVEN

CROSSING OVER

LOST HIGHWAY

Lost Highway

Richard Currey

HOUGHTON MIFFLIN COMPANY
BOSTON ◆ NEW YORK
1997

For information about this and other
Houghton Mifflin trade and reference books and
multimedia products, visit The Bookstore
at Houghton Mifflin on the World Wide Web
at http://www.hmco.com/trade/.

Library of Congress Cataloging-in-Publication Data
Currey, Richard
Lost highway / Richard Currey.
p. cm.
ISBN 0-395-52102-5
I. Title.
PS3553.U6665L67 1997
813'54—dc21 96-29724 CIP

Printed in the United States of America

Book design by Robert Overholtzer

QUM 10 9 8 7 6 5 4 3 2 1

For Aiko

Very special thanks
to Carolynn Kim-Prelutsky,
Jack Prelutsky, Lawrence Kirstein,
and Andrew Stone —
your support and faith have
been integral.

◆ ◆ ◆

And in memory of
Sam Lawrence, the great artist
of American publishing,
a life lived in
celebration of language
and books and
writers.

I was just a boy, only twenty-two,
    neither good or bad,
    just a kid like you —
and now I'm lost, too late to pray:
    I've paid the cost
    on the lost highway.

— *Leon Payne, from the song "Lost Highway,"*
written on the road, 1949

Lost Highway

Interstate 40 East, Tennessee, June 15, 1997

The road in front of me, and the night: the arbored highway a friend of sorts, passage and movement that shape the hours into something a man might accept as recognizable. In this country it is a kingdom of trees and low mountain, shadows that trace the rim of night, the road out of Nashville, cut rock and slate-face as I move uphill into darkness. I will drive toward daylight, east to Knoxville before turning north, into the Cumberlands and Kentucky.

With my left arm at a flat angle I can hold the face of my watch in the light and see the time, twenty-two minutes before midnight. The road at this hour is silent, mostly so: untraveled other than by the occasional headlights that approach and meet and pass before the dark restores and distance unites. Inside the coming distance I will turn from Lexington and cross the river into West Virginia and a world built on memory collapsing into the present, abandoned farmhouses cocked oddly under hillsides, once palatial ice-whites gone to shades of charcoal, attics given over to nesting dens for swallows and thrushes, verandas and ground floors patrolled by the local insane. Out in the emerald fields vagrant horses stand beside splintered barns, gutted back roads anchoring the meridians of a harbored universe, all returned to me under what will by then be an opening sunrise.

There was a time when I wanted to disavow my home, deny it, claim I was from a gentleman's Virginia, perhaps. West Virginia was on nobody's map of the present, in nobody's casual vocabulary, a derelict set of coordinates misplaced during the Civil War and never brought to mind again. In time I saw that all of this was true, simply accurate, and how that might be viewed was never my responsibility. I had my own troubles, beauty and loss as oddly resonant as my mother's one try at oil painting: a landscape on tent canvas, two conical mountains, winter daybreak on one peak and summer twilight on the other and a hardscrabble dirt-farm in between, our world locked into the hours and seasons, a place where time had not ceased so much as merged, all the long day's stories finally standing together.

I am a musician. Returning home from Nashville after recording an album of songs, a session that will no doubt be called a "reunion" by the childlike advertising troopers of my record company, principally owing to my age, which is now seventy-two. The fact is that every time musicians come together it is a reunion, their ages of no matter; a braided cordage, never a meeting of people so much as a confluence of impulses, desires, the rising commerce of a few separate headstrong imaginations brought together —

befuddled, eccentric, pennants of the spirit. We can call it an artist's life, but what kind of person returns to such a life on a regular basis and asks that it sustain? It is all a celebration of belief worthy of my mother's oil painting of two mountains in ice and sunlight, heat and freeze, and we are climbing those mountains, each of us, all of us, time after time.

There is not yet a title for this new album. I did not write all of the songs, although most. Fourteen titles, ten written at different points in the two years since I last recorded. Three are long-time traditional standards performed by me and many others hundreds of times, heartworn pieces — "East Virginia Blues," "Drowned in the Deep Blue Sea," and a poem of soaring regret written by a nomadic blind man shortly after World War II that he called "Lost Highway." And the new song I recorded in the last session tonight before leaving for home, composed suddenly across the previous three days, written as the other music was being recorded, between the sessions on the studio floor and while sitting on the edge of the bed in my hotel room.

I spoke into the microphone that carried my voice into the darkened control booth above the studio floor, asking the engineer for one more time. His weary voice echoed down to me through the monitors, saying he would need a moment to cue up.

I sat in the middle of the studio in a wooden chair, this last version of this last song before me, alone with my instrument and voice.

I am a self-taught musician, largely so. I play the banjo, started with a handmade when I was twelve — the year my father died — and worked my way into the music, perhaps as a defense against the ineradicable fact of his death. I composed melodies from nearly the beginning but was fif-

teen before I began to write words for my melodies, and sing them.

I waited for the engineer to cue his tape, waiting to record the song for the sixth time. It is, like many of my songs, a narrative, an account of memory's hard return when least expected, measureless, remembered by love. Someone once advised me that my songs are too often grim, preoccupied with the world's capacity to mistreat and abandon, and the question routinely follows — why? It occurred to me, waiting for the engineer's signal, that this new song was again no exception. Venerable and tireless concerns are the fullest openings into any life I know, a song nothing more than a chambered moment in the life of the heart, memory rendered with a touch of fresh energy and renewed authority.

The engineer signaled and I played the song again, sang it through to a gentle end, my voice drifting out of sight on a whisper. The playback came. I listened to the changes in the lengthening silence.

That's it, I said into the microphone. I cased my instrument and walked to the studio door and lifted my jacket from a hook. The engineer locked the booth and came down the narrow staircase that joined the studio level and we walked together through the warren of empty offices to stand in the parking lot — an easy night, the darkness high and warm, welcoming.

You staying in town tonight? the engineer asked me.

A young man, no more than twenty-five. I told him no, I'd be heading back home.

West Virginia, he said.

That's right.

The engineer gazed up into the sky and back at me and said, Pretty late to start out on the road.

I told him I'd be fine. Pleasant to drive at this hour, I said. Traffic's scarce.

The engineer looked at the asphalt. He seemed hesitant. I just need to say it's been a pleasure, he said. Working with Sapper Reeves, you know, a real privilege. A thrill, actually. I mean, I've been listening to your music since . . . well, a long time. Since I can remember. I grew up on it. You're as good as anybody ever was. But I guess you know that already.

I thanked him for the kind words and his work in the control booth, told him I hoped we might work together again, and wished him well. We shook hands, and I walked to my pickup.

I was born in coal country, my birthplace known in its locale as Waterhill Ridge, nine two-lane miles from the struggling mill town of Maxwell. My father a shaft miner like most of the fathers of that time and place, dead in the early spring of 1938 after too many years underground; my mother gone five years later in diabetic coma, a disease she never knew she had, dead beneath her painting of the two mountains in two seasons; and coming forward from that place and time, I find myself to be seventy-two. Is that old? I can ask myself such a question, having arrived at the point the question originates from. I might even smile into the thought, looking out at this highway deserted in a lost blue hour. Chevrolet pickup, half-ton. Not that I have much honest need of a truck or ever did but there is tradition in it, a certain measure of security. I like it — one rides big and high, controlled, protected. Or so it seems. Protected. There's a word, a thought, a motion in this dark. Protected from what? Surely not from time. Never from that. Not from memory. Not from legacy, or plain history. Not from oneself, least of all from that. It is never that one reaches for more than what a life holds, only that what a man sees and does defines him in all the ways he could never predict.

Near Lebanon, Tennessee. I stop to use a public restroom, buy a cup of coffee as I leave. The Styrofoam cup carries a bright cartoon of a hamburger on wheels. I ask the clerk how long ago the coffee was brewed. She looks at me, through me, tells me the pot was up when she came on for her shift.

Her voice is the edged grit one hears everywhere in mountain country. I realize I must sound this way myself.

I

Winter 1947–Summer 1950

1

AT FIRST it was a duo, Estin Wyrell and myself. We called ourselves the Still Creek Boys, the name borrowed from a gladed stream that ran beside the one-room Baptist church where I met Estin, both of us twenty-two years old. We accompanied the Sunday hymns of the congregation and practiced together in my boardinghouse room in the evenings after work nearly every other day of the week. Estin, six foot three inches with a tall man's practiced affability, another self-taught musician with the found violin he worked at a fired pitch. We played with resolute abandon, mastering enough of a repertoire to fill dancers' evenings at the local roadhouses, and it was a Saturday night in the late winter of 1947, on a break at a bar near the town of Wendell, that we met Leonard James.

Handsome Leonard. Standing beside our booth, guitar case in hand, introducing himself and asking if he could join us for a song or two. He had the perfect square face of an actor, dark eyes and eyebrows, jet hair smoothed back and shining.

Estin slipped over in the booth and Leonard sat. "You don't know it," he told us, "but I've been listening to you boys all over the county." He offered a bright smile. "And I guess you know you're not run-of-the-mill."

I looked at Estin. "The first to notice," I said. "Other than us, that is."

Estin pushed his chin toward Leonard's guitar. "I gather that's yours."

Leonard said, "Sure is. A Martin. Bought it out of a store window in Los Angeles."

"Los Angeles?" Estin said.

"Right after the war. Just got out of the Marine Corps, had a pocketful of back pay. Picked up a few chords from a fellow on the troop ship coming back from the Pacific. I liked playing, thought I'd get me a guitar of my own. Then I saw this beauty and couldn't resist."

"You learned to play on a troop ship?" I asked.

Leonard nodded. "After a fashion. A plain old six-string out of the Sears Roebuck. But when I tried a few notes on this one, I knew it was my sort of sound."

Estin took a sip of beer. "You from around here?"

"Clarksburg," Leonard said. He was diffident — a boyish charm, the flicker of risk in his eyes. He pushed his head to the left, indicating the direction of Clarksburg. "Not too far," he said. He paused, looking at us, and grinned.

"Estin?" I said. "Okay by you to try a third hand?"

"Sure," Estin said easily. "About time to get back up there, anyway."

Walking to the front of the room, I asked what song Leonard wanted to start with. "You know 'Clinch Mountain Home'?" he asked.

I told him I did.

"That's it, then," Leonard said, and he came into the song on a sliding open note, laced echo and spiraling ascent. I looked at him and he smiled with gregarious confidence, working into the song.

2

IT WAS Leonard James who coerced the loan of an aging Chrysler station wagon from his father, convinced Estin and me to resign our jobs at the hardware store and the paper mill, and we found ourselves a traveling band, without a specific destination beyond the next night, learning the music as we went, playing where we could and for what we could get. We slept together in single rooms, lined in narrow motel beds or in the parked Chrysler under roadside trees, on occasion the guests of locals, lodged in dingy third-floor rooms in the sagging houses of workingmen and their sad rail-thin wives. We played music in hotels and schoolrooms and at barn dances. We played in the garage bay of a gas station, on a river barge, standing on the bed of a pickup truck. We played at church socials and birthday parties and holiday affairs and in the undying string of roadhouses, like Tolliver's Good Time Bar and Grill, the amber heat of a hundred people pressed together on a Friday night in March 1950. The last song of the night: Leonard finished a crackling solo and drew his guitar away from the one microphone we carried with us, signaling Estin into place who burst into the song like a man fighting his own gravity. It was "Under the Double Eagle," dancers rolling loose and wild below the plywood excuse for a bandstand, older women and their men sitting in the recessed shadows where I caught the movement of heads, and Estin nodded me back into the mix. I moved to center stage, urging the song forward: three-fingered picking, nothing but motion and cornered light and a fine heat. Our faces glistened in the work of the music and we were lost in the moment's spirit until I sang the chorus another time and "Under the Double Eagle" slapped to a ringing close. The crowd cheered and called to us and asked for more, and a girl, pretty and flushed, appeared out of darkness at the edge of the platform to point happily at Leonard James.

"Any chance you'll marry me?" she shouted. Leonard went forward to kneel at the edge of the stage and shake hands with his admirer. He offered his glittering smile and she smiled in answer and they talked and after a time she drifted off with her friends, all of them satisfied customers. We began to break down and pack, disconnected the microphone, unplugged the single speaker. Estin routinely held the role of band manager and bookkeeper, and he jumped off the riser to confer with the owner.

Leonard cradled his Martin into the velour bed of its case. I closed the lid on my banjo, wrapped and tied the speaker wire, and disassembled the microphone stand, and Estin stepped back to the bandstand to call up to me. "Seems we have a small problem," he said.

I asked him what sort of problem he meant.

"The no-pay sort of problem," he said. "It seems the owner of this establishment is in fact not here at the moment. And the barkeep says he has no authority to pay the band."

"No *authority?*"

"That's what the man says, Sapper."

I knelt on the platform. "Didn't you deal with the owner when you set this up?"

Estin worked his cheek muscles, glanced back at the bartender who was cleaning up, giving us no further attention. "Well, you take people at their word. I wouldn't have put us in here if the man on the phone didn't sound right."

Leonard joined us, squatting beside me and gazing in the bartender's direction a moment before he said, "We could just rob the place." He met my eyes and added innocently, "I mean, you know, just take what we're due."

I looked over Estin's head at the bartender. A round red-haired man with the worked-over face of a manual laborer. "I suppose," I said, "we should try asking another time before doing anything rash."

Leonard shrugged.

I stepped down from the riser and approached the bar and introduced myself. I asked carefully what the problem was surrounding our fee.

"No problem that I know of," the bartender said.

"What I mean," I said, "is that we play for pay. Matter of fact, it's how we make our living. Pay the bills. Buy groceries. All that sort of thing."

The barkeep stared.

I waited, then made another attempt, slowing my voice, measuring my words. "We depend on getting paid at the end of a night. That's how it's done when you have a band in to entertain your customers."

The bartender rested his palms on the back rim of the bar. "Look, I told the tall fella there I don't know a damn about paying no band. And I gotta account for every penny going in and coming out of this register. So if I wasn't told to pay nobody, then nobody gets paid."

I weighed the chance of failure in another try, and the barkeep said, "That's about all there is to it, so you boys better get your gear and clear on out of here."

Leonard sauntered over to the bar, asking how the bartender might feel if his boss walked in and said there would be no pay for his night's labor behind the bar.

"Well, he's not walking in here and telling me that, is he?" the bartender said.

Estin leaned against the bandstand, and Leonard turned to include him. "What do you think, fellas? Figure we should just kill this son of a bitch and empty out that register?"

The few patrons still in the room sat at their tables, unsure whether they should move. A silence lowered as the bartender pressed his chin forward, cocked his head at an angle.

"He's just kidding," I said quietly.

"Funny way of joking," the bartender said. "You boys better say hello to my friend here."

"Your friend?" I said.

"Yeah," the bartender said. "Lives right here under the bar." He lifted a shotgun into view.

I looked at the bartender a moment longer and turned to walk back to the bandstand. "Come on, let's get out of here," I said.

The bartender studied us as we carried out the equipment, the twelve-gauge at port arms across his chest.

Outside, the station wagon loaded, I tossed the keys to Estin. "You up to a bit of driving?"

"Sure," Estin said. "Anywhere but here, right?"

Leonard lit a cigarette and paused before getting into the car. He looked up at the cold sky crisp with stars and a vivid crescent moon to the east. "My, my," he said, "it certainly is a beautiful night."

3

"YOU LIKE the show I put on for the bartender?" Leonard leaned forward from the back seat, bright smile shining in the dark inside the car.

"Nearly got us killed," Estin said from behind the wheel.

"Shit," Leonard said. "Those big peckers're never as hard as they look. We coulda rushed the guy, pulled that gun away from him, shot a pretty hole in the ceiling, and grabbed our money in the confusion." Leonard grinned at me, proud of his imagined scenario.

Estin said, "I can see it now. Three musicians stone cold on the floor due to an argument over fifteen dollars."

"Well, I suppose Estin has some sort of point there," Leonard said, cheery. "Fifteen bucks poorer does beat being dead. What's your view on that, Sapper?"

I turned away from Leonard to face the windshield. "I'm tired," I said.

Leonard rolled a window down an inch to flip away his spent cigarette. "Tired. You mean tonight, or in general?"

"Both."

The night split past without definition, trees hard by the roadway, flickering shades of black. Estin took the car into a long curve. "Damn thing is," he said, "we did a fine job tonight. We played real well."

"Don't fret about it, Estin," Leonard said. "Don't start that. I can't handle it when you fret."

"The thing we gotta keep in mind," Estin went on, "is that tonight was a rare thing. We gotta keep that in mind."

Leonard leaned forward to tap me on the shoulder. "Sap, he's fretting. Tell him to stop."

I spoke into the windshield. "Only the second time we got stiffed."

Estin said, "I guess that's not bad, right? Usually we get our pay. Most folks're honest."

Leonard threw himself back in the seat. "Where're we going, anyway?"

"Hartersville," Estin said.

I opened the glove box and took out the pocket notebook Estin used to keep the band's schedule. "Hartersville," I read aloud. "Volunteer fire department."

Leonard looked out on the passing night and vented a dramatic sigh. "Well," he said, "that's certainly something to look forward to."

4

TWO HOURS south of Tolliver's, Estin pulled off the road and parked.

He handed the keys across to me, drew his height out from behind the wheel and moved back to the cargo space, slipped between wheel well and instrument cases, fluffed up the pillow he kept there and pulled the door closed behind him.

Leonard was already asleep on the back seat. I edged my feet under the steering wheel and folded my jacket between my head and the door. The jacket smelled of tobacco and beer, bourbon, of distance. I tried to settle, listened to my partners' breathing. Sleep always came slowly to me on the road; even in the motels I was awake well after Estin and Leonard, staring at ceilings, watching shadows move on the water-stained walls. At times a good idea for a song came in those corners of wakefulness, fields of memory walking or the music itself, unbidden and radiant, sounding as clearly in my mind as if I were singing aloud. More often I thought of Riva, the natural logic of her body, the shape and taste of her mouth and the high curve of cheekbone sculpted to the corner of her eye. I pictured her in our little two-bedroom rent-to-own house on Delmartin Street in Maxwell, our son in the red vinyl highchair. I pictured her at night, Bobby asleep in his crib in our bedroom as she moved alone through the rooms, clearing the kitchen, turning out lights, locking up, sleeping alone.

5

THE MORNING windshield vapor-clouded, dawn chill hovering against the windows. I heard birds, fresh and closer than I thought they should be, smelled pine, and knew a door was open.

I pulled my feet to the floor, eased to a sitting position. Leonard slept on, sprawling across the back seat. I looked at my pocket watch: 7:43 A.M. I wound the stem. The wagon's back hatch stood wide. Estin nowhere in sight.

I pressed at my eyes. My face felt inflated, misshapen after the night with my right cheek against a folded jacket and an armrest. I opened the door and got out.

The morning was brilliant, the new moon still visible, opalescent, a transparent sheen. The Chrysler was parked on a curve where the highway's shoulder widened to a berm of rhododendron and man-high fern before a blunt hillside arched up and away.

Estin called to me from beyond the brush, then he was through, buckling his belt, walking toward the car. "Very pretty in there. Not at all a bad place for a man to relieve himself." He pulled up his zipper, reaching the car to bend and peer carefully through the window at Leonard. "That boy could sleep all day on a tree branch."

"Any notion how far we might be from Hartersville?" I asked.

"No clue," Estin said. "Don't guess it matters. We'll surely get there before afternoon."

"Well," I said.

"That's plenty of time to set up and be ready."

"Just that I was thinking I should call Riva, see how she's doing."

Estin leaned against the wagon. "Good idea, I guess. Check in with her. See how she's doing."

"I'm sure she's just fine," I said, knowing I sounded uncertain.

"I'm sure she is, Sapper. Not to worry. She's a strong girl, smarter than you and me put together. She knows how to take care of things. Besides, we're only out another week. Take her home a bag of money, right? Can't beat that."

I squinted against the hillside's morning shine. "Volunteer firehouse tonight?"

Estin nodded. "Bit more sedate than Tolliver's. Older folks, I imagine. And this time we'll be paid."

I studied the roadside jungle of ferns ten yards away. "I better go check your spot," I said.

"Be my guest," Estin said.

6

HARTERSVILLE, West Virginia: a main street and the storefront businesses running directly into galleried and gabled houses that stood past their prime, coal-dusted, rainswept. Estin found the firehouse without difficulty. He parked and got out and went inside.

In a few minutes he was back. "Okay," he said, slipping in behind the wheel. "Everything's set. We're due back by seven tonight. Real nice people here. They're glad to have us, I can tell."

"I'll just bet," Leonard said.

Estin let the remark pass, started the Chrysler and drove slowly the way we had come until he pulled around a corner next to a pharmacy. "Looks as good a place as any. Look okay to you?"

"Jim-dandy," Leonard said. "I need some aspirin anyway."

Estin cut the engine. Leonard went into the drugstore, returned to wash down four aspirin tablets with a mouthful of Jack Daniel's, and fell asleep again. Estin read from the encyclopedia volume he always carried on a road trip. I worked on a new lyric but stopped with the third stanza, rhymes falling away from their purpose. Children passed from time to time, coming and going from a grocery a few steps up the street. They clearly recognized us as strangers and strangely occupied — three men passing the day in an automobile. They stared unmercifully into the car. I closed my notebook and brought out my watch: a few minutes past four. I decided to find a telephone and make my call.

There was a phone booth inside the drugstore, at the far end of the soda fountain. I walked down the row of stools and into the booth to pull the folding door closed behind me. The operator put the call through and asked for fifteen cents. I dropped the coins. Riva picked up on the third ring.

"Sapper!" Her voice was fresh, breathless, as if she'd just run into the house. "It's been longer than usual."

"I know," I said. "Too long, I know. Sorry about that. It's just . . . odd hours and everything."

"Right," she said. "Those hours. But you're not working during the day. And there's those little cafés you boys stop at. You're always telling me about them."

"Riva —"

"You doing all right, Sapper? It's good to hear your voice."

"Yours too. How's Bobby?"

"He's good," she said. "And you know what?"

"What?"

"He's walking."

"You're kidding me. Already?" I settled against the bench and smiled, watching the movement of customers in the drugstore as I listened.

"Well, it's not *already*. It's time."

"I guess it must be."

"Pulled up on a cabinet door in the kitchen and just took off. He's going everywhere at a trot. You won't believe it."

"Everywhere," I said. "Walking. All over the house?"

"If I'd let him. Took his first big fall at it too. Nothing serious. A bruise."

"I guess he'll be having a lot more of those."

"I'm sure," Riva said. "But he's happy as ever. Rolling around, getting into things."

"You doing okay yourself?"

"I'm fine. Where are you?"

"Hartersville," I said. "That's not so far, is it?"

"Well," Riva said. "I suppose not. But it's not here."

The operator came back on the line, asked for an additional ten cents.

After the coin dropped Riva said, "Should we cut this short?"

"Hard to," I said.

"You have the other two with you? Are they staring at you while you make this call?"

"Not this time. They're in the car. We're just waiting for tonight. Probably get something to eat in a while."

Riva mentioned she'd had a call from the gas company — two months behind on the bill. I changed the subject with an account of the bartender and his shotgun in Wendell. I closed my eyes against the drugstore as I talked.

"My God," Riva said. "Not this again."

"This is only the second time we've been stiffed. That's not so bad."

"Wonderful," Riva said, her voice clamping. "That makes me feel so much better. My husband's been cheated out of his earnings and threatened with a firearm, but only twice." There was a moment of silence on the line before she spoke again. "Estin and Leonard okay?"

"They're fine, the usual."

"You mean Leonard's drunk more than he's sober?"

"He's okay," I said. "He's Leonard."

"Sapper?"

"Yeah."

"Just get on home safe."

"I love you, Riva. And Bobby."

"I love you too. See you back here."

On the street there were clouds riding across the town, a coming rain. The wind came up to move in my hair and I walked. At the first uphill street I turned into the climb, pavement lifting in cracked-brick abandon. I walked easily beside fences and clipped yards, striding past white houses and high porches, full-bodied black oaks and sweetgum trees shading the yards. A heavy yellow mongrel limped out in greeting. At the end of the rising street open country regained — a meadow with several Guernseys standing in a summit pasture, a picture in a frame.

I walked to the end of the street and looked.

"Pretty out there?"

I turned to the voice. An old man, easily past eighty. Waving to me from the porch of the last house before the pasture.

I waved back.

"Nice to look out there, isn't it?" the old man said. His white hair was full and neatly combed. He stood in a brown cardigan sweater over a white dress shirt buttoned to the neck. "Callworthy's," he said.

"What's that?" I asked the question from where I stood, across the street.

"The pasture belongs to Callworthy. Those are his cows. I don't think I know you. You live here in town?"

"No sir," I said, crossing the street so as not to shout. I stepped to the curb at the head of the walk and stopped, a respectable distance.

The old man looked on steadily, evaluating. "No," he said, "I never seen you before. New in town?"

"I'm a musician. I'm in town with my band. Playing tonight at your fire hall."

The old man nodded and smiled. "Waiting for things to get started out there?"

"That's it exactly. Time to kill and I thought I'd take a walk. Hope I didn't startle you."

He looked out from under his porch at the sky. "Your show's gonna get rained on, I do believe."

"No," I said, "we're indoors. The fire hall."

"Come on up here and sit if you'd like. You can see Callworthy's pasture real well from up here."

"Don't want to trouble you."

"No trouble," he said.

I walked to the porch and mounted the five steps. The old man pointed at the swing and I took the seat. The man asked what instrument I played.

"Banjo," I said.

"Well, now," he said, easing into a wicker chair opposite the swing. "Haven't heard a banjo in a time, I must say. Not living, that is. On the radio, of course."

"You know," I said, "I was just out for a walk. I don't need to intrude on you."

"You've got a good face," the old man said. "Good eyes. I wouldn't have invited you onto my porch if you didn't."

"Well, thank you," I said. "Just don't want to disturb."

"You often walk around the towns you visit?"

"Depends on the town. I just needed to get out of the car. Get a little air. And this is a nice town. Nice and quiet."

He leaned back in the chair and crossed his hands over his stomach. "Oh well, we've got our problems, the usual problems you get in any town. Any time you draw a few people together, you know. But all in all it's fine here. Quiet is what you said?"

"Yes."

"Well, sir, quiet is what you get. And I think that's a good thing for the most part. Where you from?"

"Maxwell."

The man gazed at a point in the air to the left of my face, suddenly distracted with something I could not read. Then he murmured, "Maxwell. That's upstate?"

"That's it," I said. "On the West Fork River."

"Sure," he said, looking away, out to the cows. "I've been through there. Years ago."

For a few moments we sat, not speaking, both looking toward the pasture. Then I said I should get back to the car. "My partners'll wonder what happened to me."

The old man looked back at me. "How many are you?"

"Three. Counting myself."

"Only three? You like this line of work?"

"Sure," I said. "I guess I do. There's nothing else I want to be doing, if that's what you mean."

"I always figured it was that way with you people. Music people. Circus people." His voice carried an edge of disdain. I looked again at Callworthy's cows.

The old man went on. "The kind of life you got seems so hard. Traveling all the time. No family. No roots. Why do you do it?"

"I have roots," I said, aware too late of the quickness in my voice, the seam of irritation. I took a breath and said, "I have a family. I'm married, got a little boy."

"Well, well," the man said softly. "And you out here from one town to the next."

I drew a hand across my mouth, assuming the old man meant nothing in particular, was simply taking advantage of a few minutes of conversation in the stretch of an otherwise motionless day. The luck of a passing stranger's company on a late afternoon before a summer storm.

I mentioned that I planned to be home in just another week.

"That's good," the man said, smiling at me like an unbalanced angel. "I know your wife'll enjoy that. What's your wife's name?"

"Riva," I said.

"Lovely name. You want an iced tea?"

"I really have to press on back. We'll need to get a bite before the show."

"Avery's Café," the man said with authority, leaning forward in the chair. "Right on Main Street. That's a good feed." He leaned back and the wicker creaked under the shift of weight. "At least it always was. Haven't been there for years, myself. Not since Rosalie passed on."

"Avery's," I said. "We'll look for it."

"What else you do in the circus?" the man asked. "Besides the banjo?"

I looked into his eyes, their rigid blue innocence empty and gazing, gentle as a girl's. I said that it really was time for me to go.

The old man lifted his hands from his lap, examining them as if he might read aloud from what he saw there. "It's a hard life is all, and you've got such a good face. How old are you?"

"Twenty-four."

The old man let his hands drop and gazed at me. "I'll bet you won't believe I was once that same age."

"Of course I believe it," I said.

"Those cows out there were all here when I was twenty-four. I've had to look at them all my damned life."

I waited another moment, then stood up from the swing and walked down the porch steps.

"One last thing. A word of advice from an old man. That all right?"

"Sure," I said.

"You take care of yourself. Take good care. You get to flying around up there in the air and you forget who you are. You think what you're doing is child's play, but it's not."

I looked at the old man. He delivered the words with the tone and inflection of one who knew, the fleeting undertow of life's collisions and miscalculations riding in his speech. His guileless sweet eyes betrayed nothing.

"Well," I said, "thank you, sir. Good talking to you."

"Give my best to Riva, now."

"I'll do it," I said, moving down the porch steps to the street and toward the corner. A few steps down the block, I turned to look back. The porch was empty.

7

LATE IN 1948, just before my son was born, I took the band to Charleston to record a 45rpm single, two songs. A basement studio, each musician paid fifty dollars, flat rate, no royalties. We chose a ballad of mine called "Miranda" and a quickstep dance tune we pulled together in ten minutes standing beside the station wagon, a song we generously named after ourselves, "Still Creek Breakdown." We dropped the record at backwoods radio stations when and where we could, asked the smirking disc jockeys to play at least one of the songs, and occasionally were invited to stay a few minutes and play on the air. Microphones were positioned in front of our noses and against our instruments, and on the other side of dirty plate glass the disc jockey leaned into a thin yellow light, crooning to an invisible audience *You've heard all about them they're here with us tonight the Still Creek Boys* as I reflected that in truth nobody had heard anything about us but no matter, we were there to play and did so, always one of the two songs from that first record, as if there were no other music we knew or could play or should be remembered for, and we were out and moving again, the highway a world born into the night and feeding on darkness, a town and a show, another town and a show, the nights fusing into weeks and weeks tilting oddly to months as we drummed from bar to carnival, tent shows of one sort or another, county fairs, department stores, a feed store on a Saturday afternoon and a wedding on a Saturday night, driving away into the middle of the dark and a reclaimed silence, each man adrift in whatever thoughts came. I recall a night, leaning forward to look up through the windshield, thinking I might have another sight of the full-bodied moon, and I saw nothing but ringing dark and the open spaces of sky, the weaving mesh of forest along a voiceless highway.

8

WE CROSSED the Mingo County line.

Weather trailed us downstate, migrating reefs of fog curving ridgetops and valley cuts, the brunt of traveling storms, sudden rainsqualls peppering the station wagon to slow our course into the deep mountains. We played a honky-tonk at Logan, and by the time we reached the town of Varney I remembered the whole of the long downstate journey as nothing more than a damp incandescence of early dark and cold rain blur. It was a Tuesday night, thirty minutes into the first set of the evening when I abruptly stopped playing. The song caved in around me. Estin and Leonard drifted to a halt.

Leonard asked what was wrong.

"What's wrong?" I said. "What's wrong? Look out *there.*" I pointed to a table in front where one drunk slept, head down next to a soldierly quartet of beer bottles. Several tables away two lovers entwined hands and whispered to each other. Beyond them, the bowling alley was an open-throated roar, drywood clatter of scattering pins, balls booming onto boards and thundering down the alleys.

"So it's not a good crowd," Leonard said. "Consider it a practice session."

"It might be a practice session if we could *hear* ourselves."

Estin bowed his violin once, a hostile downstroke across the strings. "So what're you saying, Sapper? That we quit and pack up?"

"Did you actually know this place was a bowling alley, Estin? When you booked it?"

Estin looked cautiously at Leonard, back to me.

"You knowingly booked us into a bowling alley?"

"Listen, Sap, the man said he had a little bar off to one side where people liked to have a drink and listen to a little music in between games. He didn't make it clear to me there was no door or anything between the bowling alley and the bar. I just took it for granted."

"You took it for granted this guy gave a damn."

Leonard stepped in. "Sapper, it's not unreasonable. You take people at their word. What else is Estin supposed to do?"

"And," Estin said, "if you're so damn good at finding places for the world-famous Still Creek Boys to play, then do it your goddamn self."

I wavered against a surge of dizziness — the blind wobble of a long series of half-slept nights in a parked car. "When I walked in here," I said, "I couldn't believe it. A damned bowling alley."

"You said that when we came in," Estin said.

"Well, now I'm saying it again."

Estin turned away from me and spoke to Leonard. "What

the hell is this? Does this man think money's easy to come by? Do you understand what he's talking about?"

A voice from behind me asked if there was a problem. The owner. "That last song sort of petered out, didn't it, boys?" He had an easy smile, an even tone. A manager at work. A negotiator.

I turned to face the man.

"Sorry," I said. "I got a little weak there. Some nausea."

The owner offered immediate concern. Did I need to sit down for a few minutes? Glass of water? How about a Bromo?

"I'll be fine," I said. "Just tired. Lot of traveling. Too much traveling."

"I'll bet that's true," the owner said, the smile fixed in place. "In your line of work." He backed away from us a few steps, bringing his hands together. "Everything's okay, then?"

I nodded, turned back to Estin and Leonard and said, "Let's try that number one more time."

I counted into the song, the owner smiling and nodding, and we played a respectable two hours with the rumble and clap of a bowling tournament, random whoops and cheers of happy bowlers, working against the melodies. During the last song of the evening the two lovers left arm in arm, having never looked in our direction. As we finished the drunk pitched out of his chair to sprawl facedown among the table legs, a wide clatter of rolling bottles and upended chairs. The Still Creek Boys packed up, and nobody rushed to help the drunk. The owner of the establishment paid in cash from a manila envelope, told us to drive safely, welcomed us back any time we might be passing through.

9

We sat side by side at the counter of Little Tee's Diner, the only customers in quiet midmorning, some twenty miles northeast of the bowling alley. The breakfast plates were cleared away and we had second cups of coffee, working away from another raw night in the station wagon. Leonard's fifth of Jack Daniel's had made the rounds a few times before we slept.

"Leonard?" I said.

"Yep?"

"Did I drive from wherever we parked to where we are right now?"

Leonard nodded seriously. "Well, Sap, you did in body. I don't know about mind. Or spirit."

Little Tee's was a strident gleam of red and white squares, flashes of chrome here and there that I found painful. The wall behind the counter a glittering array of upturned glasses and catsup bottles and stacked soup bowls. Estin pushed his coffee mug away and drew his schedule book closer. "Okay," he said. "Let's see where we are."

Leonard waved the waitress over.

"More coffee, hon?"

"You know," Leonard said to her, "I was just wondering. Are you Little Tee?"

"Nope."

"Well, it's just that we're three traveling musicians, and —"

"Like a band?"

"That's it exactly, darling." Leonard glanced at me, the mocking sideways grin. "Exactly like a band."

The waitress asked the name of the band.

Leonard told her.

She was thoughtful for a moment, then said flatly, "Never heard of you." She did not smile.

I took a sip of coffee.

Leonard threw his right hand out and open in an introductory gesture and announced, "Well, now you have."

She hesitated, frowning slightly, holding the coffeepot. "Did you say you wanted a warm-up?"

"No ma'am, I was only inquiring if you're Little Tee."

"Tee's in the back. He does the cooking. You wanna talk to him?"

I cut in. "No, we don't. My friend here was just curious."

The waitress's eyes marched between Leonard and myself, quickly to Estin, and back to Leonard. She stepped away, replaced the coffeepot on its heating rack, and leaned several feet down the counter with her back turned.

Leonard shifted close to my ear and whispered, "You take note of her chest? That's definitely a set worthy of admiration."

Estin was staring down the line, past me to Leonard. "You gentlemen care to get back to the business at hand?"

Leonard looked across to Estin, feigning schoolboy confusion. "And just what is the business at hand?"

"The rest of this piss-ant tour," Estin said.

Leonard scratched at one of his eyebrows, pursed his lips. "Estin, you take care of that stuff. Why don't you just take *care* of it? You know? And leave me out of it?"

Estin considered this, biting his lower lip.

"Fellows," I said. "My head can't stand it this morning. Estin, just tell us where we have to go."

"That's all I was trying to do."

"Okay," I said. "We're listening. You listening, Leonard?"

At this Leonard began to giggle. "I'm all ears, Sap."

Estin began to smile. He still had the faintly cross-eyed look he got when he drank too much.

I sat between them, the laughter accelerating on either side. The waitress turned to direct a hostile examination.

"We're just a bit tired," I called across to her. "Not enough sleep. Punchy."

She shrugged, turned away again.

"Okay, okay," Leonard gasped. "What was it you were saying, Estin?"

"Mudlark," Estin said.

"Mudlark?"

Now Estin's shoulders shook and he laughed silently and it took him a moment to collect his voice. "The town. The damned town."

"Mudlark?" Leonard sputtered. "Who the hell would name a town Mudlark? I never even heard of Mudlark."

Laughter erupted again. I hailed the waitress. "What do we owe you?"

She added the figures and ripped the page out of her receipt book, slapped it down beside my coffee mug.

"Four dollars, nineteen cents," she said. "And I don't see what's so funny about Mudlark."

Estin counted out the money, shoulders heaving. He raised a hand and said, "No offense, really."

We made our way out, and at the door Estin turned to say, "You give Little Tee our best wishes, now. Tell him that was a real fine breakfast."

The waitress stared. "I'm sure he'll be real happy to hear," she said.

10

I DROVE toward Mudlark, Little Tee's an hour behind us and Leonard asleep beside me, his Stetson slipping forward over his eyes. Estin slept in the back, head rolling with the motion of the road, encyclopedia volume open on his lap. The bottle of Jack Daniel's, what was left of it, cradled next to my right thigh. I glanced down at the label and the amber slosh inside, back at the highway in front, considering the skewed light falling in the wake of a fifth passed from front to back across the seat until we were no longer saddled with an actual decision to end the day. Once asleep, I dreamt of fire, embers wavering and growing to honorable and full-throated flames, honeycombed rims of jeweled heat I could see over, but only barely. I was the plainspoken witness, but it was uncertain what, if anything, was burning. I looked and studied the center of the fire and saw only a translucent mirage of working heat, a dream born in part from the night we played a honky-tonk in Kentucky only to have a drunk's cigarette set fire to a whiskey spill: the establishment reduced to a square of smoldering char within an hour.

Leonard's head fell suddenly forward, chin to chest; he snorted once and proceeded to snore. The Stetson toppled and hit the floor at his feet.

We traveled through a persistent mist that finally scattered into low-slung woodlands on either side of the highway. Midday sun streamed into the valley through wind-torn vents in the clouds, the canted topography an imprint of my boyhood — teaching myself to play the banjo on Waterhill Ridge, standing on a downslope by the creek, the world itself a thing you could hear, its own pace and grip, water and the flights of birds roaring from tree to tree. The sound of my banjo alone under high stands of locust over the hillside to the south, along the creek.

The first banjo was a gift from my mother, who traded a passing sharecropper three potatoes for the instrument and presented it to me for whatever use I might put it to. I taught myself to play with no immediate sense of how the strings worked, how a note was sounded or a chord constructed or a song built. I worked with the strings on the front porch of the house, waiting for my father to come home from the mine, painstakingly fingering down a scale, searching out the chords I needed by trial and error and the help of a twelve-page instruction book my mother mail-ordered from Chicago.

After my father's death the banjo became a refuge, and across the balance of that summer I looked for moments to slip over the crest of the ridge, out of sight of the house, where I played songs I pieced together from memory while sitting beside Redroe Creek, local music I heard — "Sweet Water Rolling," "Old Joe Clark," "The Wind Blow East." When I came back to the house, my mother, flagged by the day's work, asked me to play for her in the evenings as we sat on the front porch and looked out at the treeline, and on one evening, midsummer with the day's heat settling, I plucked a random three notes and asked her what we were going to do now that my father was gone.

She did not look at me. *I'm not sure that I know,* she said after a pause. *We'll do what we have to.*

A flock of sparrows plunged out of the treeline to turn in the air and work to the north, over the garden and the roof of the house and across the valley beyond.

Miles on and I blinked against opening sunlight and a threat of sleep, tire hum and engine noise narcotic, a sibilant drone. I slowed for a trailer rig climbing in the lane ahead. A last wisping cloud cleared the sun and vapor shredded away in the moist ravines.

11

LEONARD DREW the Chrysler up to the fence in front of my house on Delmartin Street. It was after midnight: Riva had left a lamp in the living room burning, but the rest of the house was dark. I went to the rear of the station wagon to retrieve banjo and suitcase, leaned in to say goodnight, and closed the door.

On the front porch I tried the door to find it open and Riva coming from the bedroom wearing my bathrobe. I put my suitcase and banjo on the floor and she was in my arms, simply holding me, the good smell of her hair in my face. I crossed my arms over her back, embraced her there, remembering that her back was the first beckoning aspect of her I had truly seen, in Hubble's grocery store, the summer of 1946 and a wild rain blowing against the windows. She came in flushed and already dripping and her face shining with the suddenness of the downpour. She caught her breath, smoothed water from her cheeks and hair, and turned to face the rain.

She stood, arms folded across her chest, waiting out the storm in a soaked print dress, the blossoms patterned on the dress falling along the strong curve of her shoulder blades and the smooth planes of her spine. I edged around the store pretending to have an interest in items that would allow me to draw her face into view another time, fished among the candy bars, pushed a can of soup along a dusty inch of shelf. The sound of rain eased on the roof. Selection made, I carried it to the cash register and took a casual glance to my rear. She was gone, as quickly as she had come, and I thought again of that moment I always considered our first meeting as I held her, kissing her ear and the side of her neck, the press of her breasts and length of her body full against me as we stood and held each other, spring chill folding in through the open door.

After I saw Riva that first time in the grocery store, my mind was full of her. I looked for her reappearance, asked after her around town while trying to appear innocent and uninvolved. I saw her again after nearly three months, at a dance I was playing with a pickup group that included a church organist trying her hand on mandolin, a fourteen-year-old girl with a dulcimer, and a coal miner who played a representative guitar. It was a weekend dance with families and small children and the old ones who stepped carefully around the floor in no semblance of rhythm and smiled graciously at each other after each song finished, proffering gentle bows or a few hearty handclaps, and Riva emerged unexpectedly from the crowd to walk confidently across to the bandstand.

She waved to me from the edge of the riser and I stepped closer. She asked if she might make a request.

I must have stared for a moment; she asked if I was all right. Oh yes, I said, just fine. I pointed at the musicians behind me, saying they might have trouble with a spontaneous request.

Riva said she was thinking of "Long Black Veil."

A song I loved, and I told her so. I'd have to do it myself, I said. Solo.

Riva said that would be fine, adding quickly that it was really for her father, the song being a particular favorite of his. She pointed across the room to an old man seated near the wall with a black fedora resting on his knees. He nodded to me in a courtly manner.

I looked back at Riva and she introduced herself. I said that I was Sapper Reeves, extended my hand, and she took it and said that everybody in Maxwell knew who I was.

I stood and advised the crowd that we had a special request and I performed it alone, a ghost story and a love story and desperately sad, and as I finished Riva's father lifted his hat in acknowledgment.

Then the dance was ending, families slipping into coats and gathering toward the door, and Riva came to thank me. I told her she was welcome, that I hoped her father enjoyed the song, and I abruptly heard myself ask if I might see her again sometime. She surprised me with the focus of her gaze, her hazel eyes so lucid against my reserve. She considered directly without saying a word, and if I had allowed any doubt about the pure effectiveness of her beauty it was dispelled standing there in front of her in the Maxwell grange hall.

We met again, at first simply for a walk from Riva's father's house on Greene Street across town to Vallette's Café, with that first walk folding into the miles we came to cover, owning the town in a way I had never considered: the topmost steps of the courthouse, in between the colonnades; a particularly verdant corner of grass on the grade school lawn; in front of a lilac hedge in the small square of city park; the south end of the plank bench in front of Hubble's store. The simple clean drive in Riva's personality — the clarity in her face — forced my natural reticence and gauged itself against my restraint, her intensity and resolute attention at times more than I could fully respond to. We exchanged histories, in chapters across weeks: the death of our mothers, sending me at large into the world and leaving Riva and her sister responsible for their aging and progressively more senile father. Riva's brother gone in the navy, her tiresome job in Maxwell's dingy tailor shop, my day-labor job at the paper mill and living at Mary Craigan's boardinghouse, playing banjo for all comers on the veranda through the summers until the meeting with Estin sent us into the surrounding country, a pair of local musicians willing to play for any event that might require a musical backdrop. Riva's gestures and the cast of her face as we talked were unconstrained by the enforced privacy of self I had invented and lived within since my mother died. She had discovered in some way I had not a surety of vision, an abiding resilience, a sense that what we had, what any of us had, was life as it should be.

We walked to the river in the afternoons. A gladed point set above the watercourse, shadowed by massive red oak and tangled hedges of hazelnut and rhododendron. We sat together watching the water, cut-bank eddies and riffles, the gutted hull of an abandoned rowboat shoved into brush on the opposite shore. The river ran wide and slow, we talked or were silent, watching the water, and as Riva turned to me and drew my jaw closer to her and kissed me I took her face in my hands, my thumbs tracing the edges of her mouth, around the arc of her chin and along the angle of neckline down to shoulders and arms, across her breasts. I turned her into my lap to kiss her cheeks and closed eyes, her lips, and out on the water a fish shadowed up to feed, the hollow click of water opening and closing, and above us a single bird called from the long reaches of an oak.

12

WE MARRIED in a simple ceremony at the church where Estin and I had met, at the end of a yellow dirt road beside the meandering Still Creek, on a Saturday morning. The church a single room, a solitary building at the base of a rounded hill, whitewashed with a gabled roof, an outhouse to the rear nestled in a tight stand of mayberry. Our friends from town were all in attendance, and Riva's father sat sternly in the front pew, handsomely decked out in the manner of a turn-of-the-century businessman: hightop black leather shoes, vest, watch fob, cane balanced between his knees. Estin served as best man, Leonard standing behind with that bemused expression he reserved for moments he loved.

We gathered in the pasture across the road from the church after the ceremony. Covered dishes were spread on two board tables under a maple: cold fried chicken, potato salad, green beans with hocks, peaches, corn relish. Leonard generated a theatrical event around the making of ice cream, parking two early-model automobiles side by side at a precise distance so the cast-iron freezer could be balanced on a plank set between the running boards, delegating children to the task at hand, helping the younger ones turn the big handle, grandly directing others in the stoking of ice and salt as if he were managing a steel mill. Riva's father finished his meal and was escorted to a straight-backed chair in the shade where he held court, presiding as guests came to shake his hand and leaned to speak close to his ear, and nodding as they gripped his shoulder and moved on.

Estin proposed the wedding toast, a speech praising Riva at length before noting my attributes as musician and friend *destined for greatness in his realm. I've seen him and lived with him at his worst moments, I think I can say, and watched him persevere, so I guess if he can bring that to his marriage, then a fine and wonderful woman like Riva might actually be able to stand him.*

In the late afternoon a thunderstorm collected over the hill. The wind began to rise. Tables were cleared and guests said goodbye and wished us well before climbing into cars parked at random along the pasture's rise. Mary Craigan drove me and Riva and on the trip I looked back through the rear window of Mary's Plymouth: receding church, the line of trees and tombstones patterning the green hillside, the wide-armed lift of cloud that silvered, roiled, climbed east. Riva slipped her hand into mine and I turned from the window to look at her, the radiance of her skin and faceted shadow along her cheeks. I leaned down to kiss her as storm light filtered into the car, the rain arriving to meet us as we turned onto the hard-surface road and gained speed for Maxwell.

13

RIVA CLOSED the bedroom door so as not to wake the baby and sat with me in the kitchen.

"You want some tea?" she asked.

"A glass of water'll be fine."

"Tired?"

"Pretty much. This trip seemed harder."

"I could tell when you called."

I shrugged.

"Everything going okay between you and Leonard and Estin?"

"Oh yeah. No problem there. Small disagreements, that kind of thing. Nothing major."

"That fire in Kentucky sounded pretty major."

"Well."

Riva took a long breath. "It worries me, Sapper. I can't tell you it doesn't."

"What?"

"The road, this whole thing with the band." She looked at me.

I studied the surface of the table, and after a time I said, "I think Estin does his best. You know, finding places for us to play."

"I'm very sure he does," Riva said. She leaned across the table to kiss me. Her lips lingered against mine. After a moment she said, "We better get to bed. You might enjoy a night's rest on something other than a car seat. And with a proper partner."

14

BOBBY AWAKE, standing in the crib, looking at me. He squealed once, then stared with focused interest, waiting for reaction. "Well, now," I said quietly, "what's this." I pushed back blankets and stood to step across to the crib and lift my son clear. "God. Heavy kid, aren't you. Since I last lifted you."

I nuzzled and Bob smiled, fingering my cheeks and nose. Riva turned to us, drawing blankets up and across her shoulders. "He's grown some, hasn't he? You feel it?"

"I feel it," I said. "Big as a pony. Good thing this boy's walking — keep you from lifting him."

"You feeling better?" Riva asked.

"Better doesn't even cover it," I said, watching Bob, pursing my lips for his grave examination. "I haven't slept that well in a very long time."

Riva spoke with her eyes closed. "You fellas should be checking into motels. That much at least. Sleeping in the car can't be any good for you."

I brought Bobby back to the bed and placed him next to Riva. "Thing is, we'd end up spending most of what we make on lodging if we stayed in a motel every night."

Bob crawled closer to Riva and patted her hip as if she were a large dog. Pleased with himself, he turned to grin at me, and Riva said, "That doesn't feel like you, Sapper."

"No ma'am," I said. "Younger. Much younger."

I sat in a chair at the kitchen table and gave Bob his bottle. Riva worked around the two of us, making coffee, scrambling eggs. "Oh, you're going to have a fine time," she said. "Chasing after that kid."

"All over the place?"

"All over. But it looks like it's gonna be a nice day. You two should go out somewhere."

Bob finished his bottle, managed to balance it upright on the tray of his chair, and followed his mother's movements uncertainly around the kitchen. He reached again for his bottle, knocked it rolling across the floor.

"You want more?" I said to Bob, then to Riva, "You think he wants more?"

"He might want it, but that's enough. He can have a little of these eggs when they're ready."

I put Bob on the floor; he whipped away at a wild crawl to the chair opposite and pulled himself standing to drum on the chair seat. After a second at the chair he turned for a wavering survey of the expanse of kitchen and lurched away, navigating the linoleum free-form, one wobbling step into another until with the last few he lost all equilibrium and bounded against Riva's legs where she stood in front of the stove.

I slipped down to the kitchen floor and urged Bobby to walk to me. He came bundling back, careened to fall face-first and laughing into my lap. I turned him to sit on my left thigh. "You know," I said to Riva, "I've lost track of what day this is. Sunday?"

"Saturday," Riva said without turning around. "Gas company's open until noon. Time to get a payment in."

"I'll do it," I said.

Riva brought the eggs to the table. "I'll take care of it," she said. "I'm going to check in on Daddy, I'll just drop the payment while I'm out."

I looked at Bob, feigning a small conspiracy. "It's you and me, pal. Let's see if we can get into some trouble."

Riva left after breakfast. Bob and I moved to the living room to chase each other around the furniture, hide-and-seek at the edges of the sofa. I contorted my face and barked like a dog, rolled a rubber ball back and forth, and by the time the mail came we were deep in the study of a set of picture books, accordion books with glossy trumpets, alphabet blocks, spotted horses and elephants and tigers and circus clowns. Bob pointed soberly at objects and animals. I quietly recited the names. *Dog, cow. Truck, farmer, cat.* I heard the step of the mailman on the porch and the rattle of letters going into the box.

A past-due from the electric company. A postcard from Riva's brother, now stationed aboard a destroyer in San Diego. An envelope addressed to me, forwarded through the one-man recording studio in Charleston that had produced the Still Creek Boys' single more than a year earlier. The return address was WWVA, a radio station in Wheeling.

15

WE SAT together at the kitchen table, Estin and Leonard and myself. Riva put out cups of coffee and Bobby sat on Leonard's lap, twisting one of the mother-of-pearl buttons on Leonard's shirt.

I said I'd received a letter we should certainly discuss, attempting to give the announcement a measure of gravity.

"Riva," Leonard said, "have you seen this mysterious letter?"

"I have," she said, and smiled. "Just read it, Sapper. Quit holding everyone in suspense."

"Or just hold off until Christmas," Leonard said. "Wrap it in red paper."

I took the letter from its envelope and read aloud. *"Dear Mr. Sapper Reeves, we are in receipt of a copy of the recent release from Hilltopper Records by your combo the Still Creek Boys. We think both songs show great promise. Please call me at the above number at your earliest convenience to discuss an appearance on our* World's Original Jamboree *ra-*

dio show at a date in the near future. Sincerely, A. R. Burriss, Producer."

Estin and Leonard stared at me for several seconds, expressionless. Then Estin said, "Let me see that."

I pushed the letter into the center of the table. Estin read it through and handed the sheet of paper to Leonard. *"World's Original Jamboree,"* he said quietly. "I learned about half the songs I know listening to that show."

"We *all* learned half the songs we know listening to that show," Leonard said, handing the letter back to me. "What kind of an audience you suppose they've got? Thousands?"

"More like hundreds of thousands," Estin said.

"Strange," I said. "That what you play could be heard by that many."

"Well," Leonard said, "I don't know about strange, but it sure will be different."

Riva put a cup of coffee into place for herself and sat down as Leonard told her he doubted we had played for more than a hundred people at any given time.

Estin was sure there had been more at some point.

Leonard looked across at Estin. "All right," he said, "a hundred and two."

"Does it matter how many you play for?" Riva asked. "You just stand up and play, right?" She looked firmly around the table. "What does it matter how many are listening? Your music is your music."

"Well," Estin said, "I sure as hell hope so." He turned to me. "You know, Sapper, I can't help but notice that letter made no mention of how much we'll be paid."

"I'm sure I'll hear about that when I call this guy Burriss," I said.

"God knows," Estin said, "this one we'd do for free."

"Speak for yourself," Leonard said.

Summer 1950–Autumn 1952

1

WE ARRIVED in Wheeling delayed by city traffic, then lost in a haze of one-way streets with Estin confused and agitated behind the wheel. When we finally gathered in the entry lobby at WWVA we were uneasy, intimidated and restive, clustering in front of a reception desk where a nameplate identified the young woman sitting there as simply LINDA. She looked up in firm disinterest.

"The Still Creek Boys," Leonard declaimed, reaching for a celebratory style.

Linda betrayed nothing. "You're late," she said.

I leaned forward. "Got lost," I said, polite.

Linda advised us to wait where we stood and stepped through a swinging door marked STAFF ONLY. Leonard watched her go. The door banged shut behind her and he said, "Not bad. You boys taking note?"

Estin moved to the wall for a closer study of the array of

portraits, autographed and mounted in silver frames. Hank Williams in performance, standing alone with his lips touching the microphone, eyes squeezed shut in the song's intensity. Wilma Lee and Stoney Cooper in a parlor shot with their daughter and the family dog. Doc Williams and his Border Riders, amiable in rodeo garb.

"Estin?" Leonard said.

"What?"

"I asked did you take note of that young lady?"

"Cut it out for once, Leonard," I said. "Just pay attention."

Leonard shrugged and grinned. "I *am* paying attention, Sapper."

Linda returned, stood in the doorway. "Come on back," she said.

We followed her through the swinging door, away from the crisp light of the reception area, along a darker corridor. Ahead in the distance an animated glow, the spill of channeled shadows and a fading edge of applause, a spray of laughter, an amplified voice booming.

Linda led us into an office. Mr. Burriss, she said, would be along directly. She stepped out briskly. After she was gone Leonard said, "That body's working overtime, let me tell you."

"I don't think she likes us much," Estin said.

Leonard was saying we should give her the benefit of the doubt when A. R. Burriss brushed into the office, smoking a cigar, trailing a rift of smoke. Bald, with an off-white shirt, brick-red necktie and matching suspenders. He weighed more than he needed to. He stepped around to stand behind his desk. "Still Water Boys?"

"Still Creek," I said.

"Right, well, whatever you call yourselves, you're late."

Burriss talked fast, flustered or on the verge of anger, or simply a habit of the business he was in.

I apologized, saying we had never driven in Wheeling before, and Burriss cut me short with a raised hand.

"I don't need the story of your life." He paused, staring at us as if he were looking at a picture on a wall that annoyed him. "What I had to do, gentlemen, I had to move the Texas Saddle Pals into your slot. They're on the air right now."

"Jesus Christ," Leonard said. "You're telling us we're off the show?"

"No, lucky for you. Since you're here, you'll go on where the Saddle Pals were originally slotted. But it's no way to start off. It's something you should think about. Why would you wanna get off on the wrong foot with A. R. Burriss?"

"We're not on the wrong foot," I said. "We got lost. It wasn't on purpose."

"Damn thing about you newcomers, you all think you're Hank from the get-go." Burriss tapped ash into a coffee cup on his desk. The silence weighed a moment before he barked, nearly shouting, "Which of you's the banjo player?"

I told him I was.

"Walk with me." Burriss came around the desk, taking my elbow to steer me into the hallway. We moved out of the office and into the corridor, Estin and Leonard following.

"You're a hell of a player, son," Burriss said. "You could be as good as Earl Scruggs. As good as Uncle Dave Macon. I listened to that record you boys made. A cut above the crowd, no question about it." He put the cigar in his mouth and glanced at me and away again. "You understand what I'm saying here?"

"Thank you very much —"

"Don't *thank* me," Burriss said, "I didn't teach you to play.

But I know a damned genius when I hear one." He jammed a thumb over his shoulder. "Those two boys with you are no lightweights, either. You fellas all from the same town?"

"Two of us. One from Clarksburg."

Burriss took us into a room no larger than a closet. There were instrument cases on the floor — guitar, mandolin, banjo. Burriss said, "This is where you warm up. Tune up, warm up, say your prayers, whatever you need."

I apologized another time for the lateness.

Burriss gazed at us and smoked. Then he said, "You fellas know the *Jamboree* can be heard all the way to Tulsa when the weather's right?"

"No sir," I said. "I don't think we were aware of that."

"Now you are. My point is, this is the *JAMBOREE. World's Original.*" Burriss let the point rest a moment in the air, then turned and went.

2

We were tuned and anxious when a man with a clipboard came for us. He led us out of the closet and around the last corners of the corridor, other musicians standing in half shadow along the way. Directly ahead was the stage, a high-ceilinged prospect of light bathing a quintet gathered around two standing microphones. They were in progress with a ranch ballad, singing in front of a painted backdrop depicting the interior of a barn, the barn door opening onto a hay-wagon, split-rail fence, and vaguely folded hills in an emerald distance. The man with the clipboard riffled pages. "Still Creek?"

"That's us," I said.

"You're on after the Lilly Brothers. The next act. After the Dr. Pepper commercial. But wait for your intro before you take the stage."

Leonard said that Dr. Pepper was a special favorite of his,

particularly if taken with just a dash of Jack. The man with the clipboard glanced at Leonard blankly. Then he gave us a second reminder to wait for the intro before he walked away. I positioned my banjo's neck against my chest. Estin leaned in to whisper, "Well, Sapper, here we are."

I smiled. "Yes indeed," I said. "Here we are."

3

We opened with "Miranda," playing with practiced ease, confidence and a sure grip, clean harmonies building through the song's story of love lost and regained. I looked out at the audience, row after row into the flat dark at the back of the hall, nobody moving except the bob of a head, a reflected glint of eyeglasses, the flash of a white handkerchief pressed to a face. Leonard and Estin joined me in singing the chorus, our faces side by side at the microphone, the simplicity of our voices shimmering in the breadth of the space until Estin stepped back to take the solo that soared from the frame of the song and "Miranda" rang down to its final sustained note. The applause that came was vast, and for a brief moment I was transfixed by it, the searching expanse of its sound, the pure size of it washing toward me. The three of us stood another moment before I turned to count quickly into the hard two-step of "Still Creek Breakdown," working the brisk rhythm until there was only the music in tandem, lifting a unison of big happy handclapping that pounded along in time until the band turned into that sudden moment where the song ended. The punctuated thunder of a thousand clapping hands resonated in the reaches of the auditorium after the music itself had abruptly ended: there was the moment of confusion in the audience before they realized the song was over, and they blew into wild applause.

We took a few stiff bows before an announcer in a red bow tie stepped quickly into view at the left of the stage and spoke into a microphone: *The Still Creek Boys! And now a very special word from the makers of Nestlé's Chocolate!* and we understood our time was over. The applause dissipated quickly for the commercial and we stumbled offstage and back to the closet where we had left our cases. Instruments packed, we looked at each other, uncertain whether we should simply walk back down the hall and out to the station wagon and drive back to Maxwell.

"That's it, then?" Leonard said. "Do we get a pat on the back? A go-to-hell?"

I turned both ways in the corridor. People pushed past, going in one direction or the other. "I guess I don't know," I said. "Let's head down to Burriss's office, see if he's there."

The office was empty. The music of the next act began and worked back to us, the high shiver of a pedal steel guitar echoing in the corridor. We passed through the swinging door to find the woman we had met coming in. She looked up and waited.

I took a step forward but did not speak, and she said, "What is it?"

"I guess we're finished."

"Doesn't take long." Her tone was breezy, uninvolved.

Leonard passed his guitar case from one hand to the other and said it seemed to him some sort of party was in order.

"Party?"

"You know," Leonard said, "for the performers. After the show."

For the first time she broke into a wide smile. "You're a funny one," she said.

"How so?"

"Well, there's never any party. Not that I ever heard of."

Leonard shrugged. "Just a thought."

"Was there something else you needed?"

I asked how our pay would be handled.

"Mr. Burriss have your address?"

"I'm sure he does. He should, anyway."

"Give it two weeks."

Outside, we stood together on the sidewalk, looking up at the neon letters hung against the night sky's hard indigo. *WWVA.* Blinking, on, off, orange and a livid scarlet.

"Well," Estin said, "that was certainly what you would call short and sweet."

I watched the colors of the station's call letters bumping in the air. "We got the six minutes we were promised. Just do both sides of the record, that's what Burriss said. Two songs. So we knew it wasn't any hour-long show."

"I guess," Estin said.

Leonard shifted his feet on the pavement. "We can always celebrate in the car. I got a little bit of old Uncle Jack under the seat. Let's toast our success."

We walked back to the station wagon, seven cold blocks on a dark side street. As we got into the car, a blue-eyed guard dog in a vacant lot studied us silently from behind a glinting mesh of chain link.

4

WHEN I was a boy, still learning to play, I practiced in the barn on Waterhill Ridge. The barn was my refuge in the weeks and months after my father's death, decrepit home to one tired milk cow and the leaking rafters given over to a nattering regiment of bats. Bull snakes swam the board flooring, soundless meanderings in search of mice.

A night I remember in the deep August of 1940, air heavy with the promise of rain. I carried my banjo and an oil lantern and went to meet the cow on her slow return to the barn. I put her in the stall and dropped the bar lock. The bats squeaked and warbled in the rafters, flapping out through the hay window for the night's forage. I took my banjo to the barn door, sat on a bale in the opening. From my seat I watched the kitchen window where my mother had hung a spray of wildflowers to dry, the upside-down bouquet tilting on the breeze. Sundown birds roared in the treeline and

I began to play, improvising, feeling a growth of natural strength over the strings, knowing that as my fingers moved the notes would be there, waiting, ready for me, my right thumbnail finding its place as my left hand fretted down to find an opening directly into the body of the music. I closed my eyes, hands sighting their own country on the banjo's face, a sense of place and the coming knowledge that music is traveled, borders in, rivers out. I played, a measured step on that passage, and the trees blew and whispered, notes walking one behind the other, a halftone drop and suddenly an octave above, and I sat on the bale in the open barn door, lacing the banjo's life, chanting with it, a wild rolling tangle. Eyes open again, I looked toward the valley sky beyond the house, and the music billowed under my hand as lightning flickered to the east and the wind died and the first drops of rain rattled in the trees. The hundreds of birds went suddenly silent, and the only sound still in the night was the sound of the banjo and my humming chant, and the rain came then, riveting the tin roof of the house's sagging porch and forcing me from the bale. I stood inside the barn, inside the doorway and just out of the rain, lit by the one oil lamp behind me, the roar of downpour all around as I stood and watched the water fall and played the banjo.

In the fall of 1942 I took a job at the paper mill, the principal employer in Maxwell. I worked the menial end of the labor tree — sweeper, loader, millhand's helper — and carried the banjo every day, playing for the crew at lunch, in the break room or on the loading dock. I played buck dances and backsteps, music that most of the millers knew from childhood. I accepted invitations from some other amateurs to join them playing for plates of food at family reunions and church picnics, recognizing in an unspoken way that music was my native road and best recourse, the one honest survival left even as I saw little beyond a local future — a millhand with a secret.

I worked the ten-hour days at the mill without complaint, breadwinner for my mother and myself, the two of us eating across from each other in the kitchen of the shotgun house on Waterhill Ridge, the room wood-heated and lit by two kerosene lamps.

On a night I came home late from the mill I found my mother waiting for me. I walked the cold half-mile up from the highway; there was blowing snow and a brittle wind across the ridgetop when I reached the house and my mother sitting on the bottom porch step with only a shawl across her shoulders. She had been out a time: snow dusted her hair and the tops of her legs.

I paused a few feet from where she sat. "Ma," I said, "what're you doing out here? You'll get sick."

"Needed some air, Sapper. Fresh air. Needed to smell something cold."

"You get your fill?"

"I reckon so."

"Let's go inside then, it's too cold to sit out here. It's not good for you."

I led her up the steps and across the creaking porch and into her bedroom at the back of the house. When I started to go, she asked me to get my banjo and play for her. "Pull out that chair," she said. "Play for me."

I got the banjo and pulled a cane chair into the middle of the room and sat with my back turned so she could get undressed. "Some nights I can hear you play down in the barn," she said. "It seems very far away, the way the sound travels up to me. Like hearing music from miles off. Other nights I can't hear it at all."

I nodded, facing her bedroom window. "The wind," I murmured.

"The wind?"

"It carries the music one way or the other. Some nights it's not moving uphill."

The bed whispered behind me as my mother got under her comforter. "Go on," she said, "sing for me."

"This is no singing voice," I told her.

"I've heard you singing in the barn. It's a different voice, I'll give you that. You make up those songs you play?"

I was surprised at her question, at how revealed I felt. "Yes," I said after a moment. "I do."

"Turn around here, I'm decent."

I turned the chair and scraped it across the floorboards to her bedside, and sat.

"Funny thing," she said. "I never thought that banjo would be anything more than a toy. Never really expected you'd actually learn to play."

I strummed the back of my fingertips across the strings, a light touch.

"Guess you'd rather play that thing than do most anything else, am I right?"

"Pretty near."

"Well," she said, "it's a pleasure to listen, that's a fact. What'll you sing for me?"

"My singing isn't worth much," I said.

"Thing is," my mother said, "it's how you hold back that gives your voice its heart."

I said nothing, and she smiled, patted her covers smooth. "Don't worry, Sapper, it's just us. Give me a song."

I played and sang "Old Joe Clark," but slowed it to ballad

speed, my favorite way of doing the piece. Then "The Fire Down Below," as if it were a lullaby.

My mother's eyes were closed when she spoke. "I wanted to have more children, Sapper," she said, nearly whispering. "Give you a family."

There had been a brother, stillborn, before my father died. I remembered my father hauling water for the doctor, at first the urgency between them and then the low voices, the sound of my mother crying behind a closed door.

"It didn't come to pass," she said. "What does a person do when things don't come to pass?"

I put my banjo across my lap, face up, stared down at it. "I don't know," I said.

"Then losing your father so early. Before his time. Before he'd really had a chance to live."

I waited, afraid to speak.

"He was a good man, Sapper. Gentle. A clear heart. Unusual in these mountains. He was gone too early."

She paused. The wind sang.

"One might ask why the Lord bothers. But I guess there's a good many asking the same question."

"Yes ma'am."

Then she was silent. I could not tell whether she was asleep. I listened to the weather push closer, lifting under the sky, venturing along the rivers, uphill and into our world, across our cleft of mountain and the roll of valley beyond, carrying a long night of snow against a solitary house on the side of a hill. I turned to look out the window, black light and the roar of wind filling the room, vast and breathing the both of us. Outside I saw the shapes of trees, leaning, long-haired and vanishing.

5

THE NIGHT after *World's Original Jamboree* we played a bar in Marion, Pennsylvania. We did not play well. There was a collapse in our music, the execution only ordinary, my lyrics and the energy behind them unrealized, passionless and dry. We were a band that entertained half the nation and returned the following night to a country taproom with less than twenty sour patrons at the rail and nodding in the battered chairs. I sang the final chorus of "East Virginia Blues," the tune slid to conclusion, and I unslung my banjo.

"You ready for a rest, Sap?" Leonard asked.

"Why not? Nobody out there's counting."

I stepped across to the bar and asked for a single shot of Jack Daniel's. Leonard came along and said he'd take the same. I pushed the shot down, set the glass on the bar, and asked for a second.

"First one's on the house, second you pay for," the bartender said, his voice a flat finality, a hammer meeting a nail.

I did not look up. "Deduct it from what you owe us."

The bartender slung his towel over the tap handles and poured the second.

6

LEONARD DROVE the Chrysler into a gravel lot. The roadhouse a windowless cinder-block square with a single door that had weathered several attempts at break-in. A hand-painted sign above the door, nailed to the concrete: SHERWOOD FOREST, in freehand block letters. A string of draped Christmas lights pulsing along the top of the sign, jittery pattern of blues and greens.

Leonard dipped his head to read the sign from the driver's seat. "This the place, Estin?"

"Must be."

"Where the Merry Men get together?"

"Maybe we should change our name," I said. "Just for tonight."

Leonard nodded and gave a short laugh. "The Merry Men."

Estin gazed at the front door of the roadhouse. "Got a ring to it, doesn't it? *Merry Men.*"

We sat in front of the Sherwood Forest, Chrysler idling, Leonard leaning with one arm draped over the steering wheel. No one spoke. The Christmas lights rippled.

When I turned away from my study of the sad front of the roadhouse, I sighed. "Guess we better go to work."

"Guess we better," Leonard said, pulling the station wagon to the side of the building.

Unloading equipment, Leonard looked up to Estin's height and said, "Where do you find them? Places like this?"

"I was wondering how long before one of you'd ask," Estin said.

I locked the car doors and came around to fetch my banjo. "I wasn't going to ask, Estin."

Leonard was grinning. "There a directory of some sort? A guidebook?"

Estin tucked his violin case under his arm. He managed a smile.

Leonard said he was only joking.

"Glad to hear that," Estin said. We walked, crunching gravel, and Estin added that he just liked the name. Sherwood Forest.

I nodded. "Beats Dew Drop Inn. Or Kozy Korner."

"Absolutely," Leonard said. "I can't recall any other Sherwood Forest, can you, Sap?"

"This might be the one and only," I said.

"All right," Estin said, "All right. Enough."

We pushed through the door: an open room, featureless beyond the stand of round tables and folding metal chairs. A single plank shelf behind the short bar carried four bottles, one plain brand each of gin, whiskey, rum, and vodka. The beer was served from an ice chest. A small man, balding and wearing a woman's floral apron, was unfolding metal chairs at the far end of the room.

"Not open yet, fellas," he called out. "Give me a half-hour."

Leonard said, "We're the band. Still Creek Boys."

"Oh, yeah. Hey. Come on in." The man approached; I took him to be in his late forties. The strands of his thin hair were oiled and combed straight back. "Come on in. I'm Harry Winson, this is my place. Which one of you's Estin?"

Estin nodded and Harry said, "Sure. You're the one that called me."

I asked where we were going to play.

"Wherever." Harry chuckled. "Look around, find a spot you like."

"We'll need to plug in our mike and speakers."

"Afraid not," Harry said.

"Afraid not? What do you mean?"

"No outlets." Harry pointed to the ceiling. "Just the overhead lights. No wall plugs."

I paused, looking down the room.

Estin asked about the Christmas lights outside. "Where are those plugged in?"

Harry said, "Had a line run along the outside wall for those." He tapped his forehead. "Thinking ahead."

I said, "So you had a line run outside, but none inside?"

"That's right," Harry said, nodding and smiling.

"What the hell," Leonard said. "It's a small place. Anybody wants to hear us will be able to."

I walked to the far wall and stood there for a moment before turning to look back across the room to where Estin and Leonard stood with Harry at the door. "How about right here?"

"That's it," Leonard called out. "Just where I thought we should be."

Harry bobbed in approval. "Wherever you like."

Estin and Leonard joined me. We uncased our instruments and began tuning. Harry went back to unfolding chairs, asking what kind of music we played.

"Country music," Estin said, cautious. "Country-western. I told you that on the phone."

Harry looked up from his labors. "Forgot," he said cheerily.

In due course the Sherwood Forest collected its trade, a catalogue of the local, day laborers who drove the hundred-mile round trip to Huntington five days a week, unemployed mechanics, farmers who couldn't make ends meet. We started to play and ran through our opening set as Harry Winson circulated, bringing beer from the ice chest, serving the hard liquor in shot glasses or tumblers. We were midway through "You Are My Sunshine" when the voices went up at a table near the front door.

The argument prevailed, two men shouting at each other. We looked out at the argument and at each other but kept the song moving until one of the men stood to open his coat and drew a pistol from his belt, leveled it across the table.

We stopped playing.

Nobody in the room moved — a waiting tableau of workingmen and Harry Winson in his rose-petaled apron bent over his ice chest.

The unarmed man said this wasn't fair.

The pistol looked antique, a long-barreled revolver that would have been at home among the effects of a Confederate colonel. The man holding it said he had finally taken his fill of insult.

Harry stood, wiping his hands on the apron, calling gently into the room. "Carl?"

"What?" The man answering was the one with the revolver.

"Least you can do," Harry said, "is take this outside."

"What's the difference," Carl said, "if I kill him here or outside?"

Harry said, "For one thing, the cleanup's a lot easier outside."

Carl appeared to think about this.

The man at gunpoint said again that this was unfair, a mismatch. He would, he said, be perfectly willing to settle this fairly. He'd fight, fists or guns or broken bottles or whatever, but it had to be an even contest, and Harry Winson said, "That's something to think about, Carl."

Another long moment, and Carl put the pistol on the table. He spoke to the man across from him, his voice steady and quiet and even. "Hear this, you son of a bitching piece of catshit. I'll see you outside and kill you with my bare hands. It's all the same in the end."

The man called Carl shoved back his chair with the backs of his legs and stomped out.

The other man followed.

No more than a minute passed before everybody except Harry Winson was outside, in the parking lot. Harry looked at us and shrugged.

I said, "Were we in the middle of a song here? Or was I dreaming?"

"You must have been dreaming," Leonard said.

Estin stooped to rest his fiddle in its case.

Harry approached the band, apologizing. "Those two guys have been trying to kill each other for a couple years now."

"I think we should go out and watch the fight," Leonard said. "Get our fair share of the entertainment."

I looked at Harry. "Are we going to be paid for tonight?"

Harry lifted his eyebrows. "Consider this a break," he said.

"Everybody'll be back in. You boys got a full night ahead of you."

"Even if one of those characters kills the other one?"

Harry said, "One way or another, it'll reach a conclusion. Then everybody'll be back in. They were all enjoying your music, too. I could tell."

Estin smiled, a politician on the stump. "Thank you kindly, sir," he said. "We aim to please."

"Tell you what," Harry said. "A drink on the house for each of you. What'll it be?"

I sat with Estin at one of the tables. We had beers. Leonard downed a quick punch of whiskey and went outside with the rest. I told Estin he could go too if he wanted.

"Being that these little interruptions are routine in so many of the fine establishments that engage us, I'll decline your offer, Sapper."

I smiled. "Don't go hard on yourself, Estin," I said. "I guess this is just all there is. This kind of place."

Estin took a swallow of his beer and said, "Leonard rides me too hard."

"I know he does," I said. "I'll talk to him."

"You'll *talk* to him? You'll talk to Leonard James. That's a good one."

Estin's tone annoyed me. "Suggestions, then, for improving relations?" I was terse, could hear it, regretted it immediately but did not say so.

"Suggestions?" Estin said quickly. "How about you and Leonard try and do the booking. See what you come up with."

"We've covered this ground before, haven't we, Estin?"

Estin sat back in the chair, pushed a palm across his mouth. After a moment he said, "Maybe we have to keep covering it."

I leaned on my elbows. There was shouting, a mix of cheers and what sounded like cries of alarm coming from the parking lot. I told Estin I had hoped playing on the *Jamboree* might have helped, at least offered some renewed energy, given us a sense of motion.

"Six minutes, Sap. We played for six goddamn minutes. I can barely remember being there. God knows about the audience."

"That crowd liked us, though. You can't take that away."

"Look, Sap, all I'm saying is we've got ourselves into one hell of a business here. How great your songs are or how good we are as a band or how much a crowd liked us doesn't cut much ice. Shit, it cuts *no* ice."

"Are you saying you want to quit, Estin?"

Estin's eyes left my face. "I don't know. Not really. I mean, what the hell else can we do?"

I nodded, took a breath.

Estin scratched his neck. "I don't know. Maybe we're not being patient enough."

"Just a long turnaround, you think?"

"Maybe so."

I took a drink of beer and looked toward the ceiling. "'One bright day in the middle of the night,'" I recited, "'two dead men got up to fight.' You remember that one, Estin?"

"Sure do, pardner. But is this the bright day or the middle of the night?"

"Must be both," I said.

Another uplift of shouts and cheers from the parking lot, sharp catcalls and shouted encouragement marking the give-and-take of the fight until the crowd noise eased and in due course the patrons of the Sherwood Forest filed back in, flushed from cold, resuming their seats, waving to Harry for more to drink. Carl and his adversary did not return, and when Leonard pressed through to rejoin us, I asked how it had gone.

"They waled on each other a good bit, fought themselves out, and then both finally fell down, done in. Then a couple fellas threw them into a pickup truck and drove away. I got the impression this fight is something of a continuing story around here."

I finished my beer and gestured toward the far wall. "Gentlemen," I said, "shall we continue?"

We moved back to the wall and took up our instruments and played another fourteen songs, and it was Harry Winson who approached when his patronage fell to five desolate souls, recommending we close out with the next tune.

7

I STEPPED around the house with a laughing Bobby on my shoulders.

"Watch you don't hit his head coming through a doorway," Riva said.

"I'm watching," I said, bringing Bobby into the front room, lifting him clear, swinging him down to the floor.

I had been home for less than an hour. Riva sat on the sofa and talked about his various small adventures, including a rough encounter with a neighborhood cat.

"Sounds like Bobby held his own," I said.

"Oh, he did," she said, "he did. Just as feisty as that tom-cat."

I sat down beside her. "You feeling good?"

Riva shrugged. "I'm all right." She put her hand on my thigh. "Sapper, you haven't said a word about how things went in Wheeling."

"Wheeling," I said. "Right. *World's Original Jamboree.* Already seems a lifetime ago. I think we've played about twenty-five places since then."

"We all got together at Hannah Vallette's house to listen. Must have been twenty people gathered around the radio. You never sounded better."

I watched Bobby on the floor. "We did well, didn't we? I was nervous before we went on. Size of the crowd, I guess."

"Didn't show at all in the music."

"The music takes care of itself. Thank God."

"You know, your solo on 'Still Creek Breakdown' . . . well, when you finished, everybody sitting at Hannah's broke into applause. It was thrilling."

I looked at Riva and nodded, and she said, "So when do you go back?"

"Back where?"

Riva's smile faded. "The *Jamboree,* Sapper. WWVA."

I turned to look at Bobby. "I have no idea."

Riva composed her expression, stolid, prepared. "Sapper? Leonard didn't misbehave, did he?"

"No, not at all, nothing like that. Just hard to know if we'll be invited back." I kept my eyes on Bob, on his focused work on the floor with a yellow ball. "Look, Riva — it was terrific to be there. The dream come true and all that. But . . . we went up and we played. After we finished, we walked out and drove away. And that's all there was."

I felt Riva studying my face. "Nobody . . . talked to you? After you played?"

I shrugged. "You have to remember, we were filler. Keep the show moving in between the stars."

Riva was close to speaking but did not. I was aware of her studied gaze on the side of my face. I moved closer to her and slipped my arm across her shoulders. "That boy of ours is growing like a wild man," I said. "Don't you think?"

She worked at a smile and leaned her head against my shoulder.

8

THE STILL CREEK BOYS were in town for most of the winter of 1951. We played here and there along Route 50 through the late snows and into the spring, the spate of roadhouses, a hotel, a family reunion, an Elks Lodge in Parkersburg the best pay and the only good pay. Rent and the tab at Hubble's fell behind and I borrowed from Leonard's parents. Estin still lived in a rented room at Mary Craigan's, staying on against the assurance of money to come. I continued to write — as many as two new songs a week — and the band met at my house on Delmartin Street to practice and work on new material. Bob moved out of diapers and on to the miniature flannel shirts and jeans that Riva dressed him in, offering his best version of knee-bend dancing as Estin and Leonard and I sat in a half-circle in the living room and practiced. By the end of summer Estin had strung together a week's worth of dates — a wedding, a wake, two honky-tonks, and an American Legion hall, all within a hundred miles. We were on the road five days without incident, passing the nights wrapped in blankets in the Chrysler.

9

I STEPPED through the gate and up to the porch. The Chrysler drew away, to the end of Delmartin Street and out of sight. As I reached the door, Riva opened it. "You didn't need to wait up," I said.

She smiled at me. "Wanted to."

I put my suitcase and the banjo in the hallway and walked directly to the sofa and sat. "God," I said. "I'm tired."

"It's that sleeping in the car, Sapper. I've told you about that."

"Or *not* sleeping in the car. More like lying in the car. Lying there waiting for the night to pass."

Riva came to sit beside me. I leaned across to kiss her once, lightly, on the lips. "How you been?"

She nodded casually. "Good enough."

"Bobby doing okay?"

"Oh yeah, no problem. He pretty much takes care of himself. Plays along. He plays a lot now with the Bargers' little girl."

"The fat girl?"

Riva looked at me patiently. "Yes, the fat girl. Makes no difference to Bobby. He's still bigger."

"Guess so."

"Everything go well on the road?"

"No hitches, if you can believe that," I said. "Even at the honky-tonks. The usual crew of drunks, but we play through them. Me and Estin and Leonard talked more than we have been."

"Well," Riva said, "you shouldn't rush into any decisions."

I looked at her. "Not too hard to figure what we talked about, I guess."

"Sapper, I've watched you three work all winter. Sitting here in this frozen living room rehearsing every day and watching it go nowhere. It's not lost on me."

"Christ, Riva." I looked at my hands in my lap. "Who was I kidding? Maybe music's just a hobby, something to pass the time, the way I treated it when I was a kid."

"You never treated it that way, Sapper."

I exhaled and blinked. My bones felt latticed, translucent, not built for weight-bearing.

"You might have pretended it was just a little something you pulled out of a back pocket, but it was never just a hobby. It's not that kind of thing." She paused and said, her voice pitched lower, "You're talking to me here, Sapper. To Riva. Give me credit for knowing what's going on."

I closed my eyes against exhaustion's burn and my body's diffuse ache, let my head drop back against the cushion. "Sorry," I said. "But look at me, Riva — out there acting like being a fine musician will change the world if only somebody'll pay real close attention."

"If you don't play your music like it means something, then it won't mean anything." Riva was straightforward, her voice a leveled space in the room. "Doesn't matter if you're playing for pay or not. For a thousand people or six drunk farmers."

I opened my eyes and looked at her, rubbed the stubble on my cheeks and chin. "What we're *talking* about here, Riva, is making a living. Taking care of this family. And I'm not doing it. That's all there is to it. That's what it comes down to."

Bob started to cough and sputter in the bedroom, trying to wake himself. Riva stood to see about him. "Well," she said, "like I said, don't rush into any decisions."

"This is not exactly what I would call a rushed decision," I said.

"Before you give yourself up to your bad luck, you should know that somebody called while you were gone. A record producer in Nashville." She moved toward the bedroom. "He'd like to sign the band to a contract. He wants you to call him back."

I stood and followed her to the darkness at the bedroom door. She leaned over Bob, rearranging his blanket. "I wrote it all down for you," she said. "By the telephone."

10

THE MAN who called from Nashville was named Buddy Ashford. I returned his call the next morning to hear a slow open drawl, none of the angry pressure of A. R. Burriss.

Ashford allowed the conversation to take its time with pleasantries, mentioning he had heard the Still Creek Boys on the *World's Original Jamboree,* which led him in turn to the record we did in Charleston. "A midnight record," he said.

"Excuse me?"

"That's what I call those little fly-by-night efforts. You do it in a basement?"

"How'd you know?"

Ashford laughed, a sharp bark into the telephone. "That's usually it. Basement, attic, garage. Who cares? It got your music out there. Gave me a chance to hear it. Got me on the phone with old Burriss, and he tells me you're pretty much the leader of this little outfit. So anyway, Sapper — you don't mind I call you Sapper?" He did not wait for my answer before continuing. "Anyway, far as I'm concerned, putting your stuff on long play is considerably overdue. I gather you've got more than two original tunes."

"Quite a few more," I said.

"Good. Because what I've got in mind for an album is an even dozen. They don't all have to be originals, but let's say ten should be. If you've got a couple covers you wanna do, that's okay. The Still Creek Boys can help country music shake this singing cowboy thing."

"Singing cowboys?"

"You know what I mean — Gene Autry, Roy Rogers, all that horseshit. Not that those boys aren't very good at what they do, but there's gotta be room for people like yourself and that band of yours. Serious players. That fiddle player, what's his name?"

"Estin Wyrell."

"Christ, that boy can play."

"He's good."

"Good, shit. He plays like he's been to heaven and back. And that fella on guitar — he's your engine. He gets down under that breakdown and drives it. But all this brings me to something."

"What's that?"

"I think the album ought to be called *Sapper Reeves and the Still Creek Boys.*"

I hesitated. "We've always called ourselves just the Still Creek Boys."

"I'm sure you have," Ashford said. "But you're the leader of the band. Not only that, you're the . . . what can I say? You're the *presence.* The center of the thing. You follow me?

You write the music, it's your ideas, you sing the songs, your banjo leads the way. Folks ought to know who you are."

"Well," I said, "I don't suppose there'll be any big problem on that."

"Good! Let's see, what else can I tell you? Any questions?"

I was at a loss, stunned by the suddenness and ease with which the offer was spun, out of nowhere, a disembodied voice. After a moment Ashford asked if I was still on the line and I said, "Still here. Just thinking that the last conversation I had with the boys was about quitting."

"Quitting?"

"Breaking up. Going our separate ways."

Ashford laughed, as if I had said something funny. "Separate ways where? Shit, what're you three gonna do?"

I said nothing, and Ashford came back saying, "So I'm not a moment too soon, am I?" He chuckled to himself. "You know the ballad on there, the B side?"

"'Miranda.' Actually, that's the A side."

"Whatever, but it's gorgeous, purely gorgeous. And your banjo work on that tune is . . . well, it's downright amazing. You've got a style, a sound, a way of playing that's all your own. That tune should definitely be on the album. I think we can sell a few records with music like that."

"So we're coming to Nashville?"

"You are if you want to make a record in my studio. How about five hundred dollars to the band as an advance?"

"Five hundred dollars?"

"That's my offer. Plus room and board for the few days you're working down here."

"I guess we're talking business now," I said.

Ashford brayed into the phone and said, "Sapper, we've been talking business since this conversation started."

11

THE FIRST thing Buddy Ashford did was take us to a photo session: publicity glossies, he said, and the album's jacket pictures. He drove a powder-blue Cadillac El Dorado; I sat in front beside him. The interior of the car was immaculate, dashboard glimmering and the seats an oiled white leather. "Take a good look around, boys," Ashford called out heartily. "Nashville, Tennessee."

The countryside that had carried us into town was like everywhere we traveled — low wooded mountains and long valleys, highways cut through slate beds and pine and stands of old oak. Now I watched the casual grace of settled boulevards, arbored streets, crisply squared lawns. Estin said from the back that it was all very pretty, very pretty indeed.

Ashford's chuckle was mildly belligerent. "Around here, you bet. Downtown, down where the Opry plays, it's a little rougher. But it's not a bad town, considering it's a legitimate entertainment capital in this country. They don't want to hear that in New York or Los Angeles, but a fact's a fact."

Buddy Ashford nodded and smiled and handled the automobile with the smooth clarity of a chauffeur, round belly against the steering wheel, jacket fallen open to a pink silk necktie with guitars embroidered on it, snakeskin western boots with his suit pants. He turned the El Dorado onto a residential street and within a few yards parked in front of a small house, a plain white frame affair with green shingles and shutters and two young sweetgum trees aligned on either side of a concrete walk.

Leonard said, "This is where we get our pictures taken?"

"Works out of his house," Ashford said. "Best in the business. I use him for all my stuff."

We retrieved our instruments from the trunk and approached the house, the three of us in new off-the-rack suits from Chambers' department store in Maxwell. A small man came out the front door. He was smoking a cigarette and stared at us from the stoop.

Ashford walked ahead and hailed the man. "Tony! Good to see you. Say hello to the Still Creek Boys."

Tony left the cigarette between his lips and said nothing. He squinted. After a time he said, "These guys dress that way when they're onstage?"

Leonard said usually we dressed a lot worse, and Ashford chuckled.

Tony shook his head. "Where do you find these guys, Buddy? Look like three insurance agents out for a stroll."

When Ashford spoke next his voice was flatter, less patient. "Ready to get started, Tony?"

Tony turned and disappeared through the doorway.

The front room of the house stood in near darkness, empty

except for a camera on a tripod, a reflecting umbrella, and sheets of gray paper tacked to one wall. Tony brought us into the room but took no pictures at first. He had us hold our instruments as he moved us around, stood us beside each other, positioned in different combinations of sitting and standing. He studied our faces and the alignment of our bodies with an analytical air, then turned slightly away from the latest configuration to tap a fresh cigarette from his pack and light it from the nearly spent one still balanced between his lips. He turned back to stand in final evaluation, one cigarette in his mouth and one in his hand, lost in baleful reverie as we stared back at him.

Then he took the cigarette from his mouth and crushed it out, replaced it with the newly lit one, stepped quickly behind the tripod, and told us not to move.

12

We sat facing each other on metal chairs in the studio, an airless warren of half-light and microphones and electrical cordage. We drank coffee spiced with capfuls of Jack Daniel's and listened to the taped replays booming into the studio with an immediacy and power that surprised us. We played and reworked and listened until the middle of the fifth night, when the album played through in its completion and I sat back in my chair, relieved and gratified and gently awed at the symmetry and generosity and honest invention, the full heart of the music we made, no longer songs finished in the moment they ended and consigned to whatever memory passed for. Twelve songs recorded across five nights to become an almanac of months and years earning this destination, and for me in the ranges of my secrets and fervent imaginings a reconciliation, a prayerful coming to terms, a midnight revival.

Spring 1953–Autumn 1955

1

S*apper Reeves and the Still Creek Boys* was released in mid-April of 1953. I received a parcel-post package with five copies of the album and a note that simply read *Congrats, Buddy.* Riva and I put the record on immediately, her face as warm as the light spilling into the room. She closed her eyes and nodded with the ballads, lifted Bob up and around for dancing turns on the breakdowns, sang along with my voice in two-part harmony, and at the end of the second side announced the record to be beautiful and perfect, a vision. Everything, she said, I could have wanted.

2

ESTIN AND Leonard joined me for several small ceremonies of analysis, dissecting the songs, interpreting our own frequently offhand notions regarding turns of lyric and phrasing, the warp and bend of each solo effort. The three of us signed the five copies of the album we had, each keeping a copy and Leonard recommending I wrap the other two and hide them away. *Might be worth something someday,* he said behind a sly half-grin. *Never can tell.*

I listened to the record several times a week in the three months after its release, considering methods and techniques that might improve the band's sound, enrich it, deepen the range of the songs. I practiced alone on the back porch with breaks and solos and rhythmic patterns I thought I might use on a next album. I made notes, new ideas for songs, new perspectives on old subjects, and the Still Creek Boys performed piecemeal across the following months, nothing different in our lives as local musicians on the local roads, at times taking the Chrysler a hundred miles to play two hours and returning home the same night, all for ten dollars a man.

I wrote to Buddy Ashford, asking that he send copies of the album to A. R. Burriss at WWVA and a few other radio stations that could make a difference. I said that any help in finding us work on a regular basis would be much appreciated, drafting the letter at the kitchen table after Bob and Riva were asleep, my hand shadowed over the sheet of paper by the single lamp to my right. I shaped the letter as I might the lyrics of a song, reaching for tone: insistent but polite, needful but nonchalant. We were hungry, I wrote, for work and exposure, and now we had a fine record to pivot from, a beautiful point of departure. We needed only opportunity.

Weeks passed before a postcard arrived from Buddy, on vacation somewhere in the Caribbean, a cramped scrawl on the back. He wished us well.

3

LIGHT SNOWS powdered the mountains to the west. Christmas lights hung across Main Street's two intersections; merchants painted their windows with wreaths and snowmen and reindeer. In the middle of the month an old friend from the paper-mill days, a man named Arlon Gates, telephoned to say he was involved in arranging Maxwell's town celebration, Christmas Eve at the high school gymnasium. He had a promise from the mill owner to supply gifts for the children and thought it would be very nice if the Still Creek Boys might provide the music. I assured him we would be there.

On Christmas Eve I took the band through an array of carols and a few of the dance-band standards Leonard did so well on his National Steel. Arlon moderated the giveaway from my microphone until the children were exhausted, points of flush high on their cheeks and the gymnasium floor littered with wrapping paper and ribbon. I suggested we all take a break while a few volunteers swept up. I stepped down from the riser looking for Riva, and saw her occupied behind the food table, wearing a borrowed apron and filling plates for people coming down the line. I made my way to a side door for a few minutes of what I knew was a night so cold it bristled.

The door was propped open. A few older men clustered at the bottom step. Melvin Hatree hailed me from the group and stepped clear to extend a flask in my direction, his breath smoking in front of his face. I moved down into the snow and drank: raw-skinned liquor, burnished, shed brew.

Melvin smiled, gap-toothed. "Potato whiskey. Like we done in the old country."

I nodded, breathing hard across the whiskey's drawn vapor in my throat. "Back where all we had were potatoes."

Melvin took his flask back, drank, coughed. "Yessir," he said, "only potatoes." He capped the flask, slipped it into his coat pocket. Melvin was of indeterminate age, certainly past elderly. He had known my father, would occasionally ask after him when it slipped his mind that Wilson Reeves was fifteen years gone. Melvin was a long-time rock farmer given to lecturing on the rigors of failure, the sacrificial punishment in being remanded to West Virginia after the catastrophe of Ireland.

"More than potatoes this summer, Sapper, more than that."

"What're you growing this year, Melvin?"

He coughed, a ragged growl that stayed a moment. Recovered, he said, "Whatever you want, my boy. Say the word."

"Bell peppers," I said. "Red ones."

"And so it shall be," Melvin said. "You know, Sapper, only

a wizard can draw anything out of this godforsaken dirt. Thank the Lord and the cut of the moon, I am just such a man."

I grinned.

"What're you up to these days?"

I pushed my chin at the open door of the gymnasium. "I'm a musician, Melvin. That's my band you've been hearing."

"Oh, hell yes, I remember. You were always dragging that banjo around with you."

"Still do. Another swallow?"

Melvin brought the flask out and handed it across.

"Come spring, visit me in my garden. I could use a young man's help."

I took a second hot swallow as Melvin launched directly into squash and tomatoes and sweet corn: where and how he would plant, phases of the moon to watch for, the goddamn cutworms and beetles he'd shoot with a gun if it would make a difference. Across Melvin's shoulder I saw Riva come into the doorway, the brilliance of the gymnasium's lights framing her body against the glow.

I kept well to my waltz step; Riva had always been the better dancer, guiding me with the assurance of her body. Estin alone on the riser, playing "The Tennessee Waltz." Riva moved, the grace of water in flow, a fluent elegance, her excellent soft smile in place.

"How's Mr. Hatree?" she asked.

"Apparently fine," I said. "Concerned with his garden."

Riva did a firm and perfect imitation of Melvin's Irish-inflected rasp. *"Put down your corn when the moon's a quarter."*

I laughed and told her we should have her along on the

road, doing impressions between our sets. "How are you with Cagney?"

"Not as good. And my Bogart's terrible."

I whirled her through a few steps, walked her out to turn under my extended hand, and pulled her back.

"You're getting better at this," she said.

"I think it's watching all that dancing when the band's on the road. You see some fancy stuff."

Riva smiled and we danced and Estin played away from the written version of the waltz in an emotional variation, my own passing reference to being on the road casting an unexpected peal of alarm into my chest, a tender panic, each day forward purchased at risk and against the grain. If grace was random it had never been more so, and I knew only my own uncertainty about meeting the next month's rent, clearing my debt with the grocer, keeping gas coming into the house for the rest of the winter.

Estin folded his variation into the melody everyone knew, a seamless resolution. Riva and I shared turns — first her, then myself — whirling out on the polished hardwood to end in each other's arms. Estin bowed the closing note like a wistful angel. Applause came warm and large then inside the gymnasium, and he stepped back from the microphone, tipped his head, pointed at his violin as if it were magically responsible for the music that had just been made.

We regathered onstage. Looking across Leonard's shoulder, across the length of the gymnasium, I saw Bobby on the top bleacher. He had climbed to reach his right hand up to a black windowpane and hold it there, pressed against the glass. I remembered doing the same in the winters on Waterhill Ridge, standing alone at the kitchen window, the purity of cold inside my fingertips, the glass a border against a world too wide to know. Bobby turned suddenly to find me looking at him across the lit expanse of hardwood; he grinned and dropped his hand and jumped away down the laddered bleachers to dart into the crowd. The small ghost of his hand lingered on the windowpane, fingerprints freezing white, and I heard Estin's voice suddenly at my side. "Sapper, you ready?"

I turned and nodded, adjusted my strap, moved up to the microphone. I started the beat with the heel of my right foot, counted out to four, leading into the second version of "Silver Bells" that night.

4

I WAS startled when he identified himself on the phone: I'd forgotten the sound of his voice. Buddy Ashford spoke as if only a few days had passed since we had last been in touch, instead of the sixteen months since I had received his post-card from the Caribbean. He asked after the health of Estin and Leonard, about Riva and Bob, the weather in West Virginia, never waiting for answers. He enthused over a couple new bands he had recently signed that would, he said, go through the roof. I listened and waited, knowing he would engage as far as politeness carried him and quickly reach his point.

He paused, a significant two-second silence, and then he said, "Shreveport, Louisiana."

"What about it?"

"That's where the Still Creek Boys are playing next."

"Louisiana?"

"Exposure, Sapper," Buddy said. "I thought that's what you boys're looking for."

"Well, yes," I said. "But Louisiana. That's quite a distance. And our album — I mean, Buddy, it's been out, what, nearly two years?"

"Who cares? Two years, two months. Two *days,* what's the difference? This is a major radio show. On the order of WWVA, right up there with the *Original Jamboree.*"

I was confused, wanting simply to say yes, of course we'd do the show, we'd love to do it, we'd go anywhere to play. But a wedge of caution rose to meet Buddy's proposal.

"Listen, Sapper, you just might sell some records. That's the business we're in, right?"

"Louisiana, Buddy. That's gonna take what, two days? Probably three? There's motels. Food. Gas and oil. We spend what we make just getting there and back."

"This is a six-hundred-dollar payday for you and your boys. When's the last time you guys got six hundred bucks for a single show?"

"We've *never* gotten six hundred, Buddy."

"I rest my case."

"Is there anything Castle Records can do for us on the expenses?"

Buddy gave a low whistle into the phone. "You've become a businessman since I talked to you last. And that's good, don't get me wrong. It's good. As it should be. And I'd love to help you out on that, old friend, but I'll tell you, we just about broke the bank down here getting a custom-built tour bus for Cowboy Copas. I've got to recoup a little. I'm sure you understand what I'm saying here."

"All too well, Buddy."

"Got a pencil and paper? Take this down." Buddy read the

name of the program manager and the studio's street address in Shreveport. He gave me the date we were to appear — in two weeks.

"I'll talk to Estin and Leonard," I said. "We'll consider it."

"Don't hand me that shit," Buddy said, his edged aggressive chuckle in position. "You guys're going. You telling me you'd pass up an opportunity to be on national radio?"

"I'll be in touch, Buddy."

"Sapper?"

"Yes?"

"Y'all break a leg down there in Louisiana."

5

WE WENT west from Vicksburg, Estin driving with a road map stretched across the steering wheel, breaking around in his lane as he attempted to study the map and drive at the same time.

"Watch what you're doing!" Leonard shouted up from the back seat. "You're worrying me."

"Estin," I said, "give me the damned map."

"You don't understand. I've got to see where I'm going."

"Christ," Leonard mumbled. "Look out the windshield. That'll help a lot."

I leaned across to take the map. "Estin, there's only one road out of here going in our direction. Not to worry."

"I'll have a bit more of that coffee, then," Estin said. "Might keep me awake another hour or two."

I poured him a cup and passed the Thermos back to Leonard.

* * *

I took the wheel at the village of Cheniere.

Estin and Leonard were both asleep, despite the coffee, and I drove on, a billboard looming on the right, a peeling image of the crucifixion with the words JESUS WAS TOUGHER THAN NAILS, then a smaller sign advising our entry into the incorporated town of Penders, Louisiana. I slowed in the traveler's confirmed fear of local policemen, passed black children standing in front of one-room tarpapers, staring at the Chrysler as it slid through their world. The houses grew larger as I traveled on, until we reached one that was exceptional, an actual mansion of snowy colonnades and potted trees swaying on a stage-sized gallery. Ferns waved down a marbled breezeway that faded into shadow. There were stucco cherubs in flight at the eaves, and on the lawn in front an aged black man reached a pair of shears into the flanks of a blossoming tree. He wore a stained green cap, and his shears lifted gradually, prayerful, a ballad. He turned as we passed and watched the Chrysler, and slowly lifted a hand to touch two fingers to the brim of his cap.

I waved in return, curving through a string of more modest but still lavish houses and then the array of Main Street businesses and we were in countryside again, up to speed and under way for Shreveport. Far down the road daylight hung limp as smoke, and the air pouring through my open window smelled of flowers and rain.

6

THE RADIO show — *Louisiana Hayride* — was managed by a kindly man in his late fifties named Howell Lewis. He made a point of greeting us in a personal manner, shaking our hands in turn, making eye contact with each of us, asking where we had played recently and what we had on deck for the future. I made some vague comments, and Lewis spoke of his pride in the performers he was able to attract. He was willing, he told us, to trust his ear and take a risk.

We played well and solidly, two dance tunes with "Miranda" in between, a crisp and spirited and elegantly harmonized trio of songs. A stage manager took us backstage after we performed, to a long table covered with food. Other performers milled about with plates of sliced ham and potato salad and biscuits. Leonard trailed off to investigate a cowgirl duo, and Howell Lewis came around to offer congratulations on our performance. I mentioned Buddy Ashford's energetic remarks on behalf of *Louisiana Hayride* and Lewis said he certainly appreciated any help he could get, but who again was Mr. Ashford?

I glanced quickly at Estin.

"One of my people here," Lewis said, "one of the secretaries actually, brought your album in one day, insisted I take a listen. I don't know where she got it. I just assumed she bought it at one of the local stores, but maybe this Mr. Ashford sent it down. Anyway, all I know is that I put on that album of yours and didn't lift the needle until there were no more songs to hear. The Still Creek Boys are one of the best groups I've heard in a long time. Inventive. Fresh." He went on to tell us how he had called Castle Records and made his offer of six hundred dollars. "Not much for boys of your calibre, I realize," he said, "but it was the best we could manage for a new group on a first appearance. Castle accepted it without dickering, which of course was a relief, since I really wanted to have you on the show. Never did speak to this Mr. Ashford, though. Did I step on any toes?"

I said, "I'm sure you didn't, Mr. Lewis. Buddy Ashford owns the label, and I just thought maybe the two of you might have spoken."

"Hope I get the chance someday," Lewis said. "He's obviously a man of excellent musical taste." Then he shook our hands and offered a second congratulations and wished us good luck before moving away in the crowd.

7

THERE WAS a second and final royalty check from Castle Records at the end of the summer: $218.28. I broke it out, $72.76 a man, and we continued to play as we could, selling four or five records at each stop. By early spring Estin had arranged twelve engagements across fourteen days, south into the Shenandoah. We shared on the cost of handbill printing and Estin mailed batches ahead to the roadhouse managers he spoke with on the phone, asking them to post the bills in local store windows at least a day or two before we came to town. The handbills bravely identified us as "Castle Records recording artists," and routinely we arrived to find no handbills anywhere in sight.

The music trudged, captive, played by rote. Hours inside the overheated Chrysler passed in silence. The smell of Jack Daniel's — the odor of burnt wood — was habitual in the car, and the mountains we drove through were greening and spring-wet and cool.

8

WE DROVE 242 miles in a single day to reach a destination Estin had marked on his map and in the notebook, arriving shortly after five in the afternoon. Leonard drew the Chrysler into the lot of the roadhouse and we saw the abandoned building, planks nailed over the windows. A chipped and peeling board askew over the door correctly identified the location as having once been Dorland's Easy-Stop, the establishment we were booked to play that evening. I stepped out of the Chrysler before the others, closed the door, and the sound echoed through the dark and lowering trees. A bird called once from somewhere back in the forest. The sky was dull silver, full of rain.

I walked along the outer wall of the building, as if doing so were ritual enough to change what was so clearly in evidence. A fast creek ran behind the building, a rush of crystalline water moving out of the higher country above. The rear of Dorland's was a blank wall with a single door, boarded shut. A sodden trash pile heaped smashed bottles and remains of plates, shards of amber glass sprayed into gravel, mouse-gnawed handbills promoting ladies' night, two drinks for the price of one, every Tuesday.

The creek roared, splayed over stones, gushed away under the hill, and I walked around the building to the front. Leonard sat on the Chrysler's hood, leaning back on one elbow, languid, gazing into the blank sky and smoking a cigarette. Estin stood alone in the center of the parking lot, looking at Dorland's in the attitude of a lost pilgrim. I stepped past him and out to the shoulder of the deserted highway, squatted there at the point the graveled lot met macadam. There were a few drops of rain, but I knew from the face of the sky it would not be more: the rain was still an hour away, perhaps longer.

I picked up a stone, felt its gritted surface, the sense of moisture in its facets, the marbled cool. *We have finally fallen away from any purpose at all,* I heard myself thinking, the voice of my thought nearly separate from my body, a whisper descending from surrounding forest. I looked up into the dense bowers of oak, swaying only slightly with the oncoming weather, then chipped the stone across the road, into the weeds, and walked back to the car.

9

DREAMING IN a motel bed, I saw my family gathered at the kitchen table in our house in Maxwell. Riva sat across from me, her expectant perfect face shining and dark hair catching the foreign light of the dream. Bob sat to my right, smiling, his eyes waiting.

The kitchen beyond was empty — no sink, stove, refrigerator, cabinets — dark and featureless, a table and three chairs suspended, a round of empty space. Riva spoke. *Some things make sense, some don't,* she said. Bob nodded eagerly, the grin locked on, as if he understood and agreed.

From nowhere — from the black gulf beneath the table — I lifted my banjo into the air, set it in the middle of the table.

Riva did not look at the banjo, only at me. Her gaze was emotionless, uncomprehending.

I turned to look at Bob, but his chair was empty, standing vacant at the table as if it had never been occupied. I pushed the banjo a few inches closer to Riva, an offering. She studied the ghosted white of the instrument without recognition, her eyes a gentle fold of fidelity and regret.

Rolling away from the dream, I blinked into the deep shadow of the motel room. The water stains on the ceiling were the shapes of horses on the run in a strong wind. For a moment I watched them lunging, leaning toward the door, toward the world beyond. We were three abreast, Leonard peacefully asleep in the middle, Estin's length hung on the opposite ridge of mattress. I took a long breath, easing away from the dream, and slid out of bed to pull the curtain aside at the room's one window. Across the gravel lot a solitary light burned on the manager's porch. The night paled toward a milky purple, the sky rising low and streaked over the five cabins arranged in a rough crescent along Highway 17, two miles south of Ramage, West Virginia. A heavy black Buick crunched in on the gravel. The driver, a man, parked at the manager's cabin, left the car idling and stepped out. There was a woman sitting beside him. She was holding a baby.

The man moved up to the manager's door and knocked, his breath smoking in the cold. The noise of his knock ricocheted in the stiff air, echoing out to the highway; he wrapped the collar of his coat tighter against the chill. He knocked again, backed away and stood in the middle of the porch and waved to the woman in the car, and the door opened and the manager stepped out in bathrobe and pajamas.

I watched the transaction, manager leaning out to hand a key to the man and point to a cabin directly across the crescent. The man nodded thanks and got back into the Buick and brought it around full circle on the gravel. As the car turned to pass under my window I saw the face of the baby in the woman's arms, its cheek pressed against her chest, eyes soft and large in sleep with a frilled sky-blue blanket pulled high against its chin. I remembered Bob at the same age — a few weeks old — insistently sleeping in Riva's arms. *Look at him,* I said, *look at him, Riva, he's beautiful . . .*

Riva was beatific, looking down on our child, full of settled resolve, a trusting belief in her own fulfillment.

He just might grow up to be a musician, I said. I was stroking Bob's left palm; his hand clenched around my finger.

Let's not make it too hard for him before he even gets started, Riva said. She tried to smile.

I looked up at her. *Riva,* I said, *I can't tell you how sorry I am I couldn't be here when he was born. I mean, we were way the hell out there, we had those two more shows to do . . .*

Riva looked back down at Bob. *I know,* she said simply.

"Sapper?" It was Estin, head an inch above his pillow, speaking in a loud whisper. "You all right?"

I drew away from the window, let the curtain fall closed. "Yeah. Woke up and couldn't get back to sleep."

"Better give it another try," Estin said. "Got a long way to go tomorrow."

10

"COME ON, boy," Estin said, shaking my shoulder. "Out of bed. It's damn near ten o'clock."

I leaned up on one elbow. Leonard sat in the room's single chair, smoking a cigarette, coughing around the smoke. He was wearing the underwear he had slept in, staring down at his bare feet.

"Ten?" I said.

"You got it," Estin said, placing our instrument cases near the door. "We got to be in the middle of Kentucky by nightfall."

I threw back the blanket and sat on the edge of the bed. There was a hovering afterimage of dream: the kitchen, my banjo in the middle of the table, glowing as if lit from within.

"Estin," I said, "how far you think we are from home?"

Estin glanced up from packing. "A hell of a long way. Why?"

"Just a thought," I said. "Just a thought."

11

LEONARD DROVE the first leg of the day, south from Ramage under a scattered mist of metallic cloud and unfolding rain. Usually a happy talker, he steered in silence, his Stetson a low argument over his eyebrows, his jawline blurred under three days' growth of beard.

"Leonard," I said, speaking from the passenger side, "you doing okay there? Want me to spell you at the wheel?"

Leonard stared at the asphalt. "I'm all right, Sap. One of these headaches I get. Seem to do better if I just keep my eyes pointed straight ahead. Not move my eyeballs, you know?"

"I know." I turned to look back at Estin in fitful sleep on the back seat. "Estin's out," I said. "Used up all his energy being chipper this morning."

Leonard grunted. "Estin's always chipper. Wears me out."

"Maybe he had a rough night."

"You were up a bit yourself, Sap."

"Did I wake you?"

"Not really," Leonard said. "But I knew when you got up."

"Had something of a bad dream. Wanted to let it fade."

The highway was a slick of black water, rain advancing from thin spray to a steady cold wash. Leonard put on the wipers.

"Sometimes," I said, "I can get up and walk off a bad dream."

"I don't dream, far as I know," Leonard said. "I saw in *Reader's Digest,* though, that everybody dreams, whether you know it or not."

"You just don't remember your dreams," I said. "And maybe that's just fine."

"Thing I hate," Leonard said, "is this waking up with a headache. Didn't even drink too much last night. At least, I don't think I did."

We had played a wedding reception in a one-room schoolhouse on a hill above Ramage. Leonard, typically given to celebration, was restrained in keeping to a few champagne toasts. I popped open the glove box to dig out the aspirin bottle, poured out several, and handed them across.

Outside the car it was late November, a quilted sky as we passed Logan and Mt. Gay, coming up on the Kentucky line. It occurred to me that I did not know our destination.

We had a quick lunch at a crossroads café, and Estin took the wheel. Leonard moved to the back seat.

I asked Estin where we were going. He did not speak immediately. "I know you told me," I said. "But I've forgotten."

Estin was smiling.

"What?"

"I've forgotten too," he said. "You'll need to check my book. There in the glove compartment."

I left Estin's book where it was and looked out the window, slow opening country endless in its gape of empty valleys and low hooded mountains, old mountains humped together under summer and autumn and winter rain, the country unfurling, riverine, dark-forested. Towns ranked against the spires of their courthouses and churches, low-roofed general stores and clapboard schoolhouses, peeling billboards erected years earlier and abandoned, southern Pennsylvania and West Virginia, the hills of western Maryland, southern Virginia, Kentucky and Tennessee.

The wipers slapped back and forth, doing a poor job of fanning a hole in the vapor. The wet fields smoked, the weather both solace and benediction. On my side of the windshield a dead leaf caught under the blade and slid to the left, then right, left again, smearing rainwater, a veined hand waving.

Estin drove on, across Tug Fork and into the state of Kentucky. South and southwest. Rain and muted light.

12

A SHOW in a roadhouse near the town of Dilton, Kentucky.

A young man stood at the rim of the stage and called up questions to me. He was dressed in the clothes of a farmworker and was not in his right mind. He talked incessantly, pointed at me, gestured with his questions, hummed, cried out in spurts of private alarm, spoke to me again as if we were in the midst of conversation as the show went forward. Between songs, in the middle of songs. He waved his arms over his head if I did not answer or attempted to ignore him. At one point he reached up to pull at my trouser leg, asking loudly where I was born, what my name was, why he had never seen me before. I stepped back from the lip of the stage to avoid his reach, annoyed but continuing to play. He sang in demented counterpoint with the music, his voice a moaning whine, unhinged and maniacal. The listeners standing near him took no notice as he bobbed his head and rolled his eyes, arms loose and flagging in near-seizure, and as he returned to calling up questions while I tried to sing and play, I abruptly lost my temper. I stopped the song where it stood to shout into the microphone, a quick and florid demand to throw him out, a cringing blast, the squeak of feedback through our speaker more startling and disarming than anything the demented young man had done. Estin and Leonard stared at me as I looked down at the alarmed audience, quickly realizing that they tolerated the man every day of the week, on street corners, in cafés and the bus station and every other public place in Dilton. An embarrassed silence fell, only the young man murmuring and gesticulating in front of the stilled crowd, unaware of the moment around him. After a time the bartender came out from behind the bar and called the young man by name — William — and led him out of the saloon, whispering in the low comforting tones one might use with an injured animal.

I swallowed, flooded by regret and humiliation, standing in front of the young man's townspeople. The crowd stared at me, faces slack and confused, then shook their heads and shuffled toward the door.

The motel room in Dilton had a double bed and a rollaway. Estin and Leonard took the double.

I put my banjo case against the wall. None of us had spoken since leaving the roadhouse.

"I'm sorry to explode like that," I said. "I don't know what got into me."

Leonard sat in the room's one chair to pull his boots off. "Forget it, Sap. Bastard was driving us all crazy."

"That's not like me, though. I could have asked the bartender to help the kid out. Or just ignored him. Not the way I did it. I scared the hell out of everybody."

Estin shifted out of the western-cut sportcoat he favored for performing. "Bound to run into this sort of thing eventually," he said. "We're lucky we haven't seen more of it." He gazed at me as he pulled his shirt off. "You're tired, Sapper. You snapped on this one, that's all. Don't beat yourself up. Just get some rest." He turned to billow the sheet back on the double bed.

Leonard was in bed on the far side, his back to both of us. Estin sat on the edge, took his socks off and stretched out on the bed. I stood, fully dressed, in the center of the room.

Estin said, "Turn that lamp off when you're ready, Sapper."

I nodded but did not speak. I lay down on the rollaway with my clothes on, looking at the motel's ceiling: a traveler's bad wish in the blunted glow of a single lamp. I thought of Bob, growing, always growing and deep in the good sleep of boyhood, the sleep so poised and restful it secures a house at night, holds it down, keeps it safe until morning. And Riva, alone in our bed. It was easy to imagine making love to her, turning close to run my hands under her gown, my palm riding up the ridge of her hip and my fingers against the inside of her thighs, up the sweep of belly and rib cage, kissing the back of her neck at the top of her spine, and swimming suddenly into that vision was another, sharper picture, aromatic with rain: a car crash, the Still Creek Boys gone in the wreckage, a desolate highway in the middle of an abandoned night. I was shocked by the unbidden immediacy of the idea and hung there as if projected into the scene by shame, the suddenness of the image carrying the clarity and force of revelation. The fear that rivered through me was quick and broad and simple.

I listened into the room: Estin and Leonard breathing as softly and evenly as children.

I turned off the lamp.

13

IN THAT season on the road I called home from points along the way. Pay phones in truck stops as rumpled drivers stood on line behind me; standing exposed at gas station phone booths, sun and dry wind creasing the open flats of asphalt and haggard treelines, the phone to my right ear and a finger to my left to hear above the wind.

Riva as distant as the sky, as inscrutable and cryptic. She had found part-time work, waitressing at Hannah Vallette's café; Bobby stayed with her sister when she took a shift. Maxwell, she said, was claustrophobic — an absurdity, too small, ridden by gossip and petulance and spleen. The paper mill was closed, workforce laid off, the mill owner gone to Pittsburgh with his profits. Jobs were scarce, money nonexistent. The only place people went was away. Bobby was difficult to manage, troubled, headstrong and disrespectful. I listened, and Riva's voice was flat, its energy hidden. Hidden, I told myself; I did not want to use the word *lost.* I could not recall Riva's laugh, could not center my memory on the heat in her voice when she was smiling.

I hung up the phone in forgotten corridors, motel rooms, roadside rest stops. I said goodbye and Riva sometimes said goodbye and sometimes did not, the phone line going empty and blowing across the predator miles.

14

WE CAME off the road for a two-day stand-down. The end of summer, the peach light of fading days, and I came home in late afternoon to find Riva in front of the house, furiously jamming the pushmower against a jungled crush of mixed bluegrass and crab. She worked in a housedress with her apron on, her face flushed and sweat-beaded. I walked to where she struggled with the mired blades.

"Honey? What're you doing? I can do this. You could've left this for me."

She knelt to pull wet grass from the wheelbase.

"Riva?"

She stopped what she was doing but did not look at me.

I stooped, resting my banjo case in the grass. "Riva?"

"Yes."

"Honey, this is something I'd do. You just needed to wait until I got home."

"Sapper, that has become the story of my life."

"Riva — honey, let's not have this same conversation again."

"Maybe you're right about that. Because no matter how many times we have the conversation, nothing changes."

I looked away, across our yard and into the neighbor's, across the fluted eaves and mansard rooftops. The air held the first dry braid of autumn, the faintest odor of fallen apples adrift somewhere below the waning heat of the day.

I said, "I thought we had an understanding on this, Riva. That I'd keep trying just a bit longer, just give the music a few more months."

"We did," Riva said. "Have an understanding." Her voice was a guttural scrape.

I reached to touch her shoulder. She offered no response, held her eyes on the lawnmower, on the grass, the earth.

"I just don't know if I can keep on understanding for you," Riva said. "I'm running out of understanding."

"Okay," I said, "I can accept that. If you can't handle this anymore . . ."

She looked at me suddenly but she said nothing, her eyes empty of anything beyond anger.

I waited a moment before I spoke. "If you want me to quit, just say the word. I'll walk inside right now and call Leonard and Estin. We've got one more show, but I'll cancel it."

Riva's apron, one of her favorites, held an array of spoons and bowls in happy cartoon pirouettes. She let herself drop to a sitting position on the grass, pushed the apron into the hollow between her legs, and began to weep.

I reached for her but held, brought my hand back.

"I can't . . ." she said. I waited, but she did not finish.

After a moment she stood and walked into the house,

leaving me on the lawn, crouching alone with the disabled mower and a haphazard half-cut square of verdant grass. The sun was low, working down the sky. The neighborhood stood vacant around me, windows of the surrounding houses curtained and opaque with the stillness of an aging day, the final power of the light an entreaty without direction.

15

IT WAS midway into a Saturday night affair at a taproom in Larisburg, Virginia. We had a fine little dance tune I had written called "Look for Me" in full sway, music fired to the teeth and the crowd in thrall, and I signaled to repeat the entire song. We brought the melody smartly around into the opening bars for a second time, and I turned my back to the audience, moved closer to Leonard, both of us spirited and loose in the energy of the music when I saw Leonard's eyes widen at something over my shoulder and a massive weight took me from behind, brought me to the stage in a flattening sprawl, my shoulder strap snapping hard and banjo skittering off across the floorboards, the song slammed to a hard and sudden stop. There was the sour heat of breath against my cheek; I was pinned to the stage.

Leonard tried to wrestle the man away but it was clear he was not moving, and when the man abruptly cried out *Let me be!* the aberrant wilderness in his voice frightened Leonard, who stepped suddenly away, startled, before returning to kneel beside us for an attempt at coaxing. I struggled but found no leeway, my shoulders nailed, my left cheek pressed into the scuffed and dusty planks of the stage.

I worked for the calmest tone of voice I could bring to bear and asked the man if he would please let me up. He answered, speaking directly into my ear, "I want to join your band."

"Just let me up, and we'll talk," I said.

"I purely love your music," the big man slurred into my cheek.

I was having trouble breathing well. My voice labored. "Thank you very much," I said. "But I'd like to thank you properly, standing up and looking at you." Something in this motivated him, turned a key, and he rolled off my back, awkward and unbalanced.

On my feet I saw that he was dramatically large, taller than Estin and much heavier. He wobbled, footloose on a rolling deck, his arms working away from his body to maintain balance. There was a fresh stain on the front of his shirt. "I believe," he said, so drunk that his skull wobbled on his neck like a marionette's, "that I will borrow your banjo." His voice was watery and his eyes rode over my face, ajar in their sockets.

I nodded and stepped past the man to the edge of the riser. I held my arms up to quiet the buzz in the crowd and asked if this gentleman on the stage was with anybody, if there was anybody who might help us get the show moving again.

No response. Snickers from a point in the back of the room.

I spoke in measured tones, wanting to rectify my error of

temper in Dilton of a few weeks earlier. "Folks, all we want to do is give you the best music we can. That's what you're here for tonight. This gentleman has interrupted your entertainment and he's had a little too much to drink — "

My conciliatory speech ended cleanly with my head and neck snapped forward on the end of the big man's sledgehammer hand. I went forward face first over the edge of the stage; the crowd below simply stepped aside to let me fall full weight to the concrete floor. I felt the quick heat and salt of blood squirting loose from my nose and upper lip; I rolled to my back to see Leonard in midair above the stage, landing on the big man's back, the two of them collapsing to the stage and the crowd closing over me, screaming. There was a manic scraping of feet, tables and chairs going over, beer bottles shattering. People stepped on me in stampede, kicking my flanks and thighs. Somebody I never saw paused to bring a sharp boot into my waist and again into my scrotum, fisted my right ear; my head reverberated and I struck out with my feet; a pair of legs were tagged and somebody went down. I pulled to my knees, took another blunt fist to the low back, a razored kick to the left kidney, a blow to the back of my thigh. Never reaching my feet, I tried to swivel, pumping at invisible targets, thrashing arms. I struck open air and then a series of hard connections with bone and muscle, each contact a sear of pain in my knuckles and wrist.

There was a cross-block and I whipsawed, sprawled, went down. My face slick with blood, filling my nose and throat, ears roaring, one eye clotted and puffed closed. I was lifted into a sitting position, the muscles of my neck gone rubbery. I could not see.

"Come on, Sap, let's get the hell out of here." Estin's voice. He pulled me to my feet; my legs had lost all tension and even one step demanded concentrated attention. The room seemed filled with black water.

"Come on, now," Estin said. "Keep 'em moving." I swung an arm high over his shoulders and tried to walk, leaning into him. My left foot scraped behind, dead.

"Where's Leonard?" My voice came smeared and garbled.

Estin pushed through a flail of men and boys relishing the fight, a Saturday night foray, fighting each other for the sport of the moment, and he shouted over the crowd that Leonard was okay, was somehow out front with the car, waiting for us, ready to go. My one good eye wavered.

Estin was holding me up, pulling me forward. Vision and sound came then in notched windows of light and roar and I dropped my head forward to vomit a spray of blood and mucus and bile down my shirtfront and onto my shoes and Estin simply kept moving, walking through it to draw me straight toward the door which tracked closer and larger until we were through. Shoved into a seat in the Chrysler, I saw Estin's shadow cross the front of the car to get in next to me and start the engine, and we were slamming out of the lot in a hail of gravel and the hard jerk of tires biting into pavement, sharp acceleration and engine whine, the night spinning away.

II

Winter 1961

1

I WAS suddenly awake.

Listening to the night, thinking I had heard something. The rivets of the trailer I lived in sang the wind through, moaning. I sat up to reach across and pull the curtains open. The night was alive in snowfall, snow pressing across the landscape in front of a rounded light the storm seemed to hold and carry. The cars and shrubbery and bare sycamores in the trailer park stood under deep cover.

I moved to the closet to dress. Thermal underwear, a flannel shirt and sweater, jeans and workboots, coat and gloves. I stepped carefully down from the trailer, into the night.

I saw from where I stood that I was the first to move in the storm. The road out of the park was blanketed, the walkways undisturbed. The world rose around me, a ridge of dream, faceted in a fresh extremity of cold. My breath came edged. The silence was penitential.

I walked, snow creaking under my steps. A left turn at the highway, toward Maxwell. A little more than a mile.

2

ROUTE 19 became Main Street and the streetlights ribboned away, past the courthouse and over the shops and offices and the two cafés. McPherson's gas station crouched with its imitation ramparts, the garage windows a flat black and the gas pumps unrecognizable under snow.

The blizzard slanted through the streetlamps' glow, and in the quick passage through light every snowflake glittered, magnified and identifiable, countable; beyond the streetlamp a soft and breathing night, the air a powdery smudge, a drifting whirl. Rooftops and doorways and the open beds of parked pickups gathered snow and Main Street lay before me, a sweep of carpeted white, with a radiance it rarely owned.

At Davis Street I turned right off Main, down a block to Delmartin. The Websters' three-story Victorian on the corner of Davis and Delmartin swung into the storm in a confusion of shadowed angles. Wisping snow swirled along the empty porch.

The night glowed in reflected snowlight. I walked the two doors down to the house on Delmartin where Riva and Bob still lived and stood on the sidewalk in front as if I might be practicing for the solitude I kept, preparing for the nature of silence. In the near distance I heard the river moving under the snowfall, and the snow itself made a sound when I listened for it, reaching the ground in a nearly inaudible sigh.

The house sat square and plain, the porch banister holding a high cap of snow in a beautifully rounded line, one end to the other. The aluminum milk box to the right of the door had been left open and was already full of blown snow. A drift leaned against the bottom of the door; the windows were curtained, no light anywhere. Walking into town from the trailer park, I had thought that Bob might be awake, might have heard something through his sleep to signal the storm, that he might be up and excited, but I saw that the house was still.

At the end of Delmartin I turned left on Greene and walked the two blocks to Main and paused at the corner to face north, toward the silent center of Maxwell. At this hour, in this weather, I saw the street entire, the length of it leaving town at the far end in a narrowed core of disappearing light and the shrouded hills beyond, dim and impenetrable. The street was the world, the small and clean definition of the world, the lucent borders of the days and months. In the six years since the night in Larisburg when the Still Creek Boys had come to an end, I had been frightened by anything more than this, by the strained possibility that I might take to any morning and find this street somehow different, transplanted, irrevocably changed, no longer my own.

I had dreams that returned, versions of dreams: I walked out into Maxwell to find the roots of the world growing in directions I could not understand or abide; I was unknown, somehow feared. I greeted people I knew, who shied with the rarefied fear of animals, eyes wide and glassy. I walked and grew smaller, my body growing closer to the earth until the buildings reared and towered, closing away the sky, the street in front of me an open mile of concrete, cars and trucks thundering, the engines of hell.

Mornings came, daylight a form of redress against the dreams, the weathers and seasons of time a rendition of comfort, returning me to this point at the head of Main Street, which I might tack down like a photograph in an album, a page I could return to and say *Here, this is the place I come back to,* all landscape and turning world, an undernourished hope, a private translation of what might pass for desire and promise or, failing that, the thin and simple virtues of stranded luck. The night in Larisburg lingered whenever I found it in a corner of memory, the hapless fear and a final image burned home: a drunken stranger pounding my banjo to splinters and twanging wire, grinning and yelping, before Estin was beside me and speaking into my ear and pulling me to my feet.

I stood and watched the snow from the corner, the studied palpable fall. The world was its own perfected shape, bounded only by the visionary width of the sky, and I walked again, keeping to the sidewalk, the faultless snow in the street calling for a last few hours of sanctity before the morning traffic came. Past the storefronts, Marla's New and Used, Chambers' department store, Renton's For Men, the Woolworth's big-windowed menagerie of toasters and hair curlers, postcards, cheap cameras and Elvis key chains and the comical women's wigs sitting askew on faceless Styrofoam skulls.

I knocked on the front door of the house on Delmartin Street. The snowfall was lessening, and the night hovered. I invited Riva's alarm and annoyance, coming to the door at this hour with the frivolous notion that I might take my son out for a walk, but I knew Bob would be fascinated, ready at once to join me on the adventure.

I saw Bob on most weekends and a night or two during the week. He was a resilient boy, high-spirited, in many ways happier with the new living arrangement which gave him a second playground and set of friends in the trailer park where I lived.

Riva opened the door, face set hard against the disturbance until she looked beyond me and saw the night.

"My God," she murmured. "Look at this." She pushed her head through the door to look around at the neighborhood, then drew back. "Sapper," she said, nodding.

"Riva." I smiled. "Sorry to get you up, but I thought Bobby might like to come out with me, take a walk before everybody else is up and moving around."

She drew her robe closer. "I'm sure he would," she said.

I stepped in and stood like an uneasy guest. Riva went to wake Bob, returned to say that he would be along directly. "And what're you doing up at this hour, anyway?" she asked.

I told her that something had wakened me, and when I looked out, I discovered the blizzard. "I knew it would be beautiful," I said. "Thought I'd get out and have a look."

Riva nodded. We allowed a few moments to pass in silence. I heard Bob bumping about in his bedroom. "Riva," I said. I was not sure how to continue.

She looked at me, in a manner I thought might be searching. Then she said, "While you two are out there freezing to death, I'll be in bed. It's nice to sleep under a snowfall."

"That it is," I said. "If Vallette's opens this morning, I'll take Bob to breakfast."

Riva touched my arm at the elbow, then turned to her bedroom.

3

WHEN WE reached Main Street, Bob stopped for a moment, overcome by the tableau, admiring the unsullied breadth of the street. Then he merged with the snow, kicking powdered spray in front of his boots, slogging figures-of-eight into the Main Street cover, running precarious one-footed slides, loosed into his freedom, a twelve-year-old in command of his world.

He stopped at the head of the alley between Woolworth's and Lake's TV Repair, staring in. Then he called into the high-walled enclosure, *Hello?*, a compelling uncertainty in his voice. I stood beside him.

His voice echoed and returned from the snow and wet brick, a ricochet. He took a few steps into the alley and tried again. Now the echo was sharper, and Bob looked up at me, feigning fright. "Might be somebody in there," he said. "Talking back to me."

I pursed my lips in serious consideration.

"Or that's the snow," he said, looking down the alley.

"The snow?"

"Talking to me."

"The snow is talking to you?" I said.

Bob turned back to me and grinned. "Could be," he said. "Out here like this with nobody else around. That's when you can really hear."

"Well," I said, "I think you're correct about that."

Bob gave a last call to the snow before he plunged on, downtown. The eastern line of hills gained a shaded definition against the storm, a fragile blur, the sky softening under the ceiling of cloud.

"Daylight's coming," I said, but Bob was too far ahead to hear.

The first snowball took me by surprise, sailing from a doorway to catch my shoulder. I dodged back, flattened against the store window, knelt for a handful of snow, and delivered it into Bob's left shin as he appeared on the run. He darted into the street and I threw as quickly as I could. Bob stood then, in the middle of Main Street, and I watched his amused steadiness there as he looked directly at me, unsullied, a principled warrior. He patted together a snowball the size of a melon, smoothing its sides, walking toward me. I delivered precisely targeted hits into his thighs and arms and he was on me, heaving the two-pound lump into my chest. I went backward and down in a shower of ice and powder, Bob laughing and racing off, back down Main. When I caught him we were both panting. We leaned hands on our knees, laughing against our breathlessness. Daylight seeped from the sky's edges, a distant milky glow, and we stood in front of Hannah Vallette's café. Bob put his two gloved hands against the glass, leaned close to blow a smoky haze in front of his mouth.

A light went on suddenly in the back of the room.

Bob watched as Hannah emerged in coat and muffler and big dairyman's boots. She was moving forward when she saw us at the window and waved, unlocked the front door, pushed it open to ask if we had been waiting all night.

"Pretty near," Bob said.

Hannah pulled him inside. "Get in here, smart guy," she said.

"We were just out for a walk," I said. "We could come back later, give you a chance to get things going."

She waved me in. "Only fifteen minutes before I open anyway," she said, as if it were any other day. "Grab a seat. I'll get the coffee going."

We ate breakfast in the third booth back from the door. The milkman and the postmaster came in the front door and greeted Bob and me as they passed to take a booth behind us. Bob was flushed and animated, sipping at hot chocolate and turning from time to time to look out at the street and the gradual resumption of activity, shopkeepers scraping squares of sidewalk clear at their doorways, waving to each other, standing in rubber boots to talk about the storm.

Bob told me he was determined to become a police officer. A state trooper. He enjoyed uniforms.

I nodded over my coffee. "Sounds good," I said. "Reliable. Always a demand for policemen. Dangerous work, though. At least, it can be."

Bob flatly rejected the idea of danger. "That's if you don't know what you're doing," he announced around a mouthful of scrambled egg. "Proper training and you're in the know."

I looked at him. "Is that a fact?"

"Yes sir," he said.

"You've been doing some research on this?"

Bob shrugged. "Been talking to Will Buckman's dad. He's a trooper."

"That's right," I said. "I'd forgotten about that."

"Will's dad says training's the thing. He says these small-town cops don't get proper training."

I smiled. "You mean, like the force here in Maxwell."

Bob took another bite of eggs, looking at me as if I were only tolerably intelligent companionship. "Dad, if you were in big trouble, would you want Whittle on your side?"

I laughed and shook my head. Tom Whittle was somewhere past sixty years of age, floridly overweight, a long-time stalwart of our five-man Maxwell force.

"I mean, really, Dad," Bob said, "what could Officer Whittle do when the chips were down?"

"Well," I said, "it is a frightening thought, I'll grant you." I sliced into my omelette. "God help us, Bobby, let's hope the chips are never down."

Bob looked at me, earnest and supremely confident, as if no challenge could ever tax him. "Will's dad just says to expect the unexpected, is all."

I smiled and nodded, imagining the slogan on a smudged sheet of paper and tacked to a wall in some police substation. "How're your eggs?" I asked.

"Good," Bob said. "But the hot chocolate's better," he said. He lifted the mug and held it two inches from the table-top. I touched it with my coffee cup.

"Hey," Bob said, "that's like a toast."

"That's right, pardner," I said. "Here's to snow days."

4

I WALKED Bob home after breakfast. We passed the doors of Ben Sedge's hardware store, where I worked six days a week, the job inherited from Estin when he moved to Memphis to join his cousin in a dirt-hauling operation. I was not due at work for another two hours and we walked on, Bob talking urgently about the wonder of a day free from school, as if he had won a lottery. He planned his recruitment and organization of neighborhood boys for something he called his snow army. They would build igloo fortresses, he said, and wage an ice war.

I thought of the job I would do that day, had done for five years: mixing paint and directing elderly women to the seed packets and flower bulbs; sending farmers to the correct aisles for molly bolts and hatchets, toilet seats, mauls, fence-post diggers; bringing fifty-pound bags of feed and seed up to the register and appearing interested as customers paged enthusiastically through catalogues offering decorative cinder blocks and brightly colored wheelbarrows. I finished each day at Sedge's and drove to the trailer and rarely allowed myself to think about destiny, or question its existence, its variety, or the precise and fully unexpected nature of its calling. At the trailer I talked to the cat I kept — the stray that had arrived one day from its own nowhere and stayed on with authority — and poured a double Jack Daniel's, straight up in a coffee mug. I sat on a kitchen chair and drank and watched the sun fall through the open door, if there was sun on that particular day, or simply inspected the fade of light against the porthole-sized screened windows. On some nights I put on a record, Faron Young or Bill Monroe or Flatt and Scruggs. There were other nights I could not bear banjos and guitars and fiddles, hating the sound the instruments brought together, the world they came from, and on those nights I chose jazz, foreign and captivating. With a saxophone on the turntable — piano, muted trumpet — I poured a second double and waited for the fullness of dark.

We stopped for traffic at Main and Greene. Bob asked if I might be available to help him design his snowfort. I looked down at him. "I've got to work today, son. Like most days."

"You could come over tonight."

"Son, it'll be too dark tonight. Tell you what. This is Friday — you won't be at school tomorrow. And the snow will still be around. I'll come over early in the morning and we'll get a good start on it. If you and your buddies haven't finished it already."

Bob nodded, his face beaming, fresh and pink. "Sounds good," he said.

"Now put up your hood," I said. "Your mother will think I'm not taking care of you."

Spring 1961–Summer 1965

1

I PASSED a week in a country hospital after Larisburg, eyes swollen shut, my face the shade of an aging orchid. Breathing came in shallow gasps after the two fractured ribs; I was fed through a tube and urinated into a steel bottle cradled cold between my legs. Leonard was in another room, in critical condition, bleeding from the kidneys and a lung.

The first day in the hospital bed I labored in a febrile panic, infused by a desperate impulse to stand and pull out the tubes and walk away, to get back to Riva, to Bob, and when I lifted my head from the pillow the room collapsed toward me, spinning flat and loud against my eyes. Estin put through a call to Riva from the nurses' station. We would all be home as soon as Leonard and I were well enough to travel. *What did she say?* I wanted to know, the question forced through lips so distended they seemed clownish, a ridiculous mask.

Estin did not speak immediately. When he did, he said, *Not much for her to say, is there? You just get better now, pardner. Ol' Estin's right here.*

He passed from my room to Leonard's and back again, the carrier of news, progress reports, words of encouragement. He read aloud from his encyclopedia volume as my mind wandered, and told stories of his boyhood in Kentucky, the Wyrell family strung along the wrong side of a stream called the Big Sandy, trying to make do on vegetable gardens and three hogs a year stretched between eight people.

I looked toward the window as Estin talked. There was the top of a tree moving in the wind, the sky white and featureless. Estin drew me into his story, his voice animated and resonant as he told me about the Wyrells' decision to leave Kentucky after his mother died. They struck into the west, *every man's promised land,* and settled in the vicinity of Denison, Texas, where Estin passed his ninth birthday. It was a birthday he would never forget, he said, because the sand was over the tops of his shoes with every step he took.

Estin's uncle wanted to call Texas the failure it was and move the Wyrells on to California with its promise of clean water and steady work in the orchards and artichoke fields. Estin recalled his father's response: they had left a hard life to find a harder one, and if he was going to die, he was going home to do it.

I turned from the window to look at Estin, leaning forward on his chair at my bedside. He paused.

Hey, buddy, he said, *I'm just running on here, I guess. Maybe I should let you rest?*

No, I said, *your past is better than my present.*

Estin grinned.

I moistened my congealed lips. Estin went on to tell how he and his father were the only family members to come back to Kentucky. They caught a ride with an Indian into Oklahoma and jumped a freight that stopped in the middle of the night on a bridge over the Arkansas River. Thinking the peculiar stop meant railroad detectives, they ran off to hide and later found work as side-by-side egg collectors on a chicken ranch.

Estin stopped, lifted his eyes to my window. *Strange,* he murmured. *Knee-deep in chickenshit all day, sleeping on back porches and in barns at night, and it actually seems as if those were the good old days.*

After the second night in the hospital, sleep no longer came. Watery light lay along hushed corridors, over the silhouettes of my bed and bedside tray and the visitor's chair, and somewhere in the hollow distance a radio played Nat King Cole.

By the third night my eyes fully opened and the misted vision cleared and breathing came with less pain. I touched the stitch line along my right ear where the skin had been torn away from my head: a ragged embroidery of flesh to skull. The emptiness that came then consumed me, acquitted nothing and traveled nowhere, fulminant and absolute. My dead mother's voice sailed in on the convections of spirit, unheralded but heard as authentically as if she were standing in a corner of the room. I thought I heard one of the songs I had sung to her in the wind-vented bedroom on Waterhill Ridge years before, and a nurse shadowed the doorway, checking on me. The sound of my mother's voice was instantly gone; the nurse could not see that I was awake. She stood a moment, then padded away, her starched white dress sighing in the corridor.

2

A YEAR passed after Larisburg before I considered buying another banjo.

At the music store in Clarksburg I pointed to a nondescript instrument on the overhead rack; the proprietor reached it down and offered it to me. I did not handle the instrument, simply told him I would take it.

He looked at me, confused. He asked if I wouldn't like to try it first, make sure it was what I was looking for.

I told him to put it in a case and let me pay for it.

He squinted at me another moment but did as I asked.

I drove back to Maxwell with the banjo on the front seat beside me, took it into the trailer, and stood it upright in the closet.

Then I went back out to my truck and drove into town. I parked in the lot next to Woolworth's and walked two doors south to the Riverside Tavern, went in, and took a seat at the bar. I asked for a double Jack Daniel's with a beer back, and drank standing up.

I drank alone and persistently, thinking at first that I might recall my mother's voice with the same awful purity it had carried in my hospital room. That was the dawn voice of its time and place, animal bone and rain, wide torrents of snow-melt and soaked hollows and valley floors where the green was firmament, a cascading jungle of fern and rhododendron, cloaked solitude, tree-filtered sunlight and shadow-fall. It was the voice that followed me even in the days I did not hear it, a scrim of blood singing with blighted eloquence. It was the voice I imagined I could not hear.

3

I PLAYED music here and there, a few times at a rundown bar to the east of Maxwell, sitting in with a group of high school musicians. They were good enough but without the passion or sense of obligation to the music I remembered having at the same age, and I returned to my trailer missing the blaze of redemptive satisfaction inspired by a little renegade crowd bursting into applause after a ballad or dancing to euphoric exhaustion on a five-minute breakdown. After a night of playing with the teenage locals, I sat alone in the dark with the cat on my knee, afraid, the intimate fear so familiar from the final months on the road, when my life had stirred in its own dry wake and anything passing for self-knowledge had leaked away into the shrouded winter dawns and ancestral forests, unrevealed.

4

THE CORRUPTION of dreams: alcohol sheen of nights in spectral drift, the artifacts of intoxication, stunted rage and the surfacing of desiccated courage or more often only an evaporation of care, of any remaining sense of responsibility. What comes back comes in pieces, edges, scenes: weaving along the sidewalk to my truck after a night at the Riverside, hoisting myself inside to fall against the steering wheel. My forehead lodged against the horn, and I could not move. The sound of the horn filled Main Street, echoed in the alleys and the doorways of stores and shops and the open portico of the courthouse, loud and unrelenting, and I began to laugh, the laughter of unnamed desire, of mercenary hunger, and always the darkness, never drinking during the day, saving the apparition for sundown, dusk, nightfall. Two policemen — one of them the wheezing and portly Tom Whittle — tapped at my windshield, opened the truck's door to lift me away from the steering wheel.

And the night Riva bailed me out of the Maxwell City Jail for twenty-five dollars she certainly could not afford, drove me to the trailer as I hung in stupefied nod on the seat beside her. She helped me up the trailer's three steps to the door, where she launched me into the dark interior, as if she were cutting a boat loose from a mooring, shoving the hulk away into the black.

5

THERE WAS a night that I went to the Riverside with the modest intention of having a few drinks and regained consciousness at the end of the alley between Woolworth's and Lake's TV Repair. My elbows were abraded, the right thigh of my work trousers torn and blood-streaked. I was vomit-soiled and oil-smeared from where I had fallen. I had no memory of leaving the bar or making my way into the alley, or why I did so. I sat up with my back propped on the brick wall and looked into the vent of night sky between the buildings. My head lurched and eyes ached. I fought a tide of nausea.

The stars burned in a cold and resolute space, white and blue, pulses flickering across an empty night. Main Street was silent at the end of the alley. A gentle rise of wind brushed the rooftops, but there was no movement of air in my warren of trashcans and used lumber heaped into the cul-de-sac of the alley. I got to my feet.

My truck was stolidly parked where I had left it — the only vehicle on the deserted street — and I passed by. I was too depleted to do more than walk, thinking I might return to some manner of resilience in the walking itself, focusing on the aluminum square of my trailer as home, destination, belief. I passed the places defined for me by Riva, vivid in their innocence, their ordinary and essential plainness: a bench, a step, a corner of public grass. Quiet and unadorned places, no different from generic points of reference in any town of similar size and intent, but places I had once owned in the good clean air of Riva's mind, the strength and welcome in her face.

I stood on a corner, looking toward the invisible river, thinking of Estin's advice to simply let go, to abandon what he called *your private war.* He called me every few weeks from Memphis, usually late at night; we exchanged visits at least once a year. *This is moral injury,* he told me once, *and there's no rescue for that, my friend. You accept it and move on.* Perhaps so, I thought: the last dream of hard portent, where sanctuary is only a harbinger. I sheltered in what I could see, the restrained local distances and the buffer of time, and told myself to wait, be patient, that in the fold of years I might come to have perspective if not actual understanding, if I never came to even a tentative peace with my mind and what had gone before.

I turned to walk again, singing a phrase to myself. *Down the road,* a fragment I sang as a boy, coming home from the paper mill, pressing up the mired track to the house on Waterhill Ridge, *down the road to the land beyond.* The words were first in my head, in my inner ear, when I was fourteen or fifteen years old, and I sang them looking for the melody to fit in those seasons adrift through the high arms of oak and box elder and sycamore; words and a scrap of melody riding before there was any palpable sense of myself as more than a boy walking home from a day's hard labor. That song never grew beyond those few words, its tag of melody heard again in a thousand private moments since I heard it for the first time, in and out of sleep, under my breath in the Chrysler traveling from one town to another, at work stocking the back shelves of the hardware store. A few words and ten seconds of music that resonated on the ledges of memory as if its meaning hovered at the core of my life.

I passed the sign that marked the city limit of Maxwell. The two lanes ahead pulled to the north and faded into darkness, and I knew it was not the fragment of song that mattered but all that came below it, the weight that no song holds in itself but points toward and signifies, all the traveling voices that whisper and chant in hiding. We wait out our lives, the frightened children and bereft prisoners of those voices, waiting to speak until we forget how or what it is we must say, until we find ourselves standing alone and dreaming on an empty road.

6

It was in the summer of 1965, shortly after dusk on a Saturday, that Estin came to the door of my trailer with a new banjo.

There was predictable conversation about the long drive from Memphis, which I allowed to be unnecessary but Estin insisted was no problem for him, given the importance of what he carried. He ducked into the trailer, being nearly too tall to stand erect inside, glanced about for a place to rest the case, and put it down on the half-sofa arranged against the end of the room. He unlatched the case and opened the lid.

It was a gloriously beautiful instrument — a Gibson Mastertone, the fittings and gold plate capturing light, the fret board with its filigreed mother-of-pearl inlay and the interior of the case lined in vibrant blue velvet.

"Happy birthday," Estin said.

I looked at the banjo and at Estin. "It's not my birthday," I said.

Estin shrugged. "My mistake. I never could remember your birthday."

I looked back at the banjo with my customary difficulty in finding words to meet the moment. After a time I stepped backward and away and sat in the recliner opposite the sofa.

Estin pushed his hands in his pockets and stared at me. "If it doesn't satisfy, I'll return it and get another."

"It's not that, Estin," I said. "You know it's not that."

"Then get over here and pick this damn thing up and play it."

"You know you didn't need to do this," I said.

"On the contrary, old friend. I came to understand that this was one thing I had to do." He paused, watching me. The top of his head hovered an inch from the ceiling.

I moved back to the sofa and lifted the banjo out of its case. The instrument's balance was precisely engineered, the grip oiled and smooth. I returned to the recliner and sat forward on the edge of the seat with the banjo balanced on my right thigh. I ran my thumb down the strings, brought them into tune. Then I played a soft and measured "Fire Down Below."

We listened to the sculptured fade of the music until there was silence, and we listened then to the silence. After a moment Estin cleared his throat and said he would make some coffee. I started to rise and he waved me back. "You play, Sapper. That's all you have to do. You just sit there and play."

He stepped into the kitchen. "I got my fiddle out in the car," he said casually. "I'll fetch it here directly and we'll see how we sound. Where do you keep the coffee?"

We played together until past midnight, as many songs as we remembered, and the next morning took my truck into town and ate breakfast at Vallette's. As we finished our coffees, Estin suggested a walk along the river.

We passed the abandoned paper mill, most of its windows broken and the loading docks littered with blown trash. I took Estin across the weed-covered grounds, stepped over the rail spur, and cut down toward the river.

We picked our way along the wooded bank, water slicing into view through the trees, the hulk of a coal barge tied on the opposite side, rusted out and vined over. The lower banks were crowded with black walnut and shoulder-high rhododendron; where the bank met the water we walked, downstream. Estin asked after Bobby.

"He's good," I said. "A virtual pillar of strength, that boy."

Estin nodded. "Always was, if you think about it. Long as I can remember, a boy with his own straightforward take on the world."

"Sixteen years old now."

"Hard to believe."

"That it is, Estin."

"And Riva?"

I did not answer immediately.

"You two see each other?"

"We run into one another, if that's what you mean."

"Fine woman."

"Definitely that," I said.

"Wish I'd been that lucky," Estin said.

"You still seeing your secretary?"

"She quit."

"What, the job or you?"

Estin laughed. "Both."

The path narrowed. I stepped in front and we pressed under a lush overhang of willow. The path opened out to a small vantage at the water, a few feet above the current. We stopped and looked out at the river. A cloud-hidden sun, the birds slow in the high branches around us, their songs drowsy, the air close and warm.

"Hope you like that banjo," Estin said after a time.

"*Like* doesn't come close to how I feel about it," I said.

Estin looked at the ground, pursed his lips, and looked up again to focus somewhere on the tangled flank of the river's opposite bank. "You and Riva ever consider getting back together?"

The smell of the afternoon was everywhere, verdant decay of river mud and the redolent green of the forest around us. "Well . . ." I started.

Estin waited for me to continue, and when I did not he said, "It could be you're sitting on something here that's outlived its usefulness, Sapper. I know the depth of your disappointment, because I was part of it. We did what we could, that's all."

He paused and I sensed his eyes on me. I watched the barge rise and fall on the current, as if the river were breathing. "And I gather you believe," he continued, "that you have disappointed Riva in some way that can't be repaired. But it just might be a pain that's no longer worth the investment. That's getting too old to accurately recall."

"I recall it," I said flatly.

"Okay," Estin said, "okay." He lifted his hands and let them drop again to his side and shrugged. "I don't mean to meddle." He waited a moment, then said, "You know, we weren't so far off the track all those years ago — kids playing music when and where we could. We got in trouble thinking there was more to it than that. We just held on too long."

"I guess," I said.

"Look, Sap, you're a hardware clerk and I got a little dump-truck outfit. That doesn't mean we aren't musicians. It doesn't mean you can't be with the woman who I know you love and who I think still loves you. So you messed up, got lost for a bit — we were all on that same road. We all shared the risk. It hurt us all, one way or another."

I watched the flux and spin and press of the river, the train of water with its surprising weight and quiet velocity, the driven logic of blood. There was an insistent vibration in my chest and my lips shook, eyes filled. I angled my face away from Estin, and we stood side by side on the river's edge in a dry welter of oak and bamboo, shifting our weight on the mud, pretending to study the motion of the water and the rising shape of the day.

Summer 1966–Winter 1967

1

FROM DOWN in the brake came the sound of a single shot. After a moment Bob was beating up the side of the hill, bright-faced and grinning. "I did it," he called out. "Took it right down with one shot." He was breathless when he reached my side.

I asked him what it was that went down so easy.

"Deer," he puffed. "A big doe."

"Well, then," I said, "we'll be eating well."

"Yes sir," Bob said. He was proud of himself.

I looked down the hillside, toward the thicket where Bob had been. "We better get down there. Make sure the animal's out of its misery."

"Just an old deer," Bob said, tracking beside me in the meadowgrass, his rifle cocked over his shoulder.

I considered an answer and thought better of it; this was my son, now seventeen and never one to worry much about the sadder creatures of this life or the wreckage a man might leave in his wake. Bob was a happy boy.

He pushed ahead, leading me to the kill. She was full-sized, lying on a bed of leaves, her flank round and fur as smooth and shining as if it had been recently brushed. Bob nudged her with the toe of one boot.

I looked up into a cross of wild gold and brown and shimmering green, all the trees of the season. It was late in the day and I turned to the east. "How far you think it is back to the truck?" I asked.

Bob clicked his tongue, considering. "A mile, easy."

"Well," I told him, "we'd better get to it or we'll lose the day. Let's lash her to a pole and get rolling."

I never carried a rifle. I had no interest in hunting, but Bob was ready for a firearm from the time he understood the concept of blood sport, had always been the boy to creep around the side of the house and ambush me with a vocal rendition of gunfire. He would kill me over and over and race off, out of sight, sometimes alone and sometimes with his friends, half of them set out in Western regalia. Bob remained confused in those years as to why I was not a cowboy myself, with so many country-music performers invested in lizard-skin boots and elaborately decorated shirts with rhinestone-studded panels. Then there was Roy Rogers on grainy Saturday morning television, the only kind of country musician Bob knew about: a man who chased a band of hombres into a hardscrabble canyon, pinged a few shots into the rocks before he had the drop on the bad boys and carried them to a righteous justice, wrapping up his day with a sweet little tune back at the ranch, a rack of oily-haired crooners balanced four abreast on a hitching rail to one side.

When Bob was young — five, six years old — he watched

the television screen with Leonard James's Stetson riding down his forehead, but it was not the music he took note of. It was the shooting. After a show he strapped on his holster and galloped an imaginary horse around the yard and I know in his mind he was somewhere in Arizona, hard by the Mexican border, in the saddle down in an arroyo, that big stallion's shoes clattering and sliding over open rock.

"You doing okay there?" Bob called to me from his place at the rear of our carry-pole.

"Fine so far," I said. "This is where we learn how long a mile is."

The sun was in the trees, the light falling quickly. The pole creaked as the deer swung on the lashes and we trudged, going on without talking. After a time I began to lose my sense of comfort about the hour and the precise distance we had to go, and I suggested that perhaps we'd walked past the trailhead.

We stopped. "Maybe so," Bob said, winded from the carry. He gazed up into the darkening trees overhead. The sky was still a husky blue.

He lowered his end slowly and I let my end down. I reached in to touch the animal's chest. "Certainly don't want to lose this meat," I said.

"We're not going to lose her," Bob told me. "We got time." He was studying the woods ahead. "Seems like the way we came in, but I guess I'm not sure."

I was annoyed as much as worried. "Damn thing is," I said, "I don't know if we've gone too far or not far enough."

Bob grinned at me with no particular feeling in either direction. "Reckon we spend the night here?" he said, teasing me, laughing.

"Sleeping with this deer of yours?"

He shrugged, kneeling beside the doe.

I sat down to lean against a tree trunk. "Is that it, then? A night on the cold ground?"

There was enough light to see Bob's wide smile. "Wouldn't hurt us. We could cook up a little of this deer for supper." He pushed at my knee, playful, hoping to reassure.

"What a couple of damned woodsmen we are," I said. "We'd have been hopeless failures as pioneers."

Bob said he should scout around a little. "We're probably right on top of the trail, can't see it for looking."

I considered. "If we get separated out here, we'll have a real situation on our hands." There was a blade of agitation focusing under my ribs. I should have paid attention to the length of the shadows. Riva would be on the phone to the Highway Patrol if I did not have Bob at her front door on Delmartin Street within another two hours. I looked across at my son: he was stretched out on the ground, hands tucked behind his head as if he were at home in his own bed.

"You ever lie like this and look up into the trees?" he asked. "It's very peaceful."

"Bobby," I said, "don't get too comfortable. I'd like to at least try and get home tonight."

Bob pulled up to one elbow and told me I should be an expert at this kind of problem in view of the stories I told about getting lost with the Still Creek Boys, driving dazed and hopelessly confounded in towns with three streets. He grinned and stood up.

"Listen," he said, "I'll just go up and down a bit, get a bearing. If I don't come up with anything, you do the same. One of us can wait here. That way we won't get separated."

"Makes sense," I said.

"If we passed the trail, it can't be far back. And if it's ahead, it's just around the corner."

"Watch your footing," I said. "It's already too dark to see the ground."

"I'll just yell if I need you. We'll use voices to stay in touch." Bob marched off in the direction we'd come from.

I patted the big doe beside me. Still warm. In a moment the dusk seemed full of music, owls, rabbit scratch, mocking-birds, nightingales. I looked down at the earth between my knees, a square of dry leaf and scuffed soil. *We'll use voices to stay in touch.* What I wanted to do for much of my life, what any musician, any singer, any songwriter, wants to do. What any animal wants to do. A natural impulse, the desire to turn one's life into a song of some sort, to allow that singing to mark the life, to chart its prophecies, its destinations. The forest was all Bob's music, the plain walk into every new day, his secret freedom. At times I thought I might envy men with the capacity to live without regret, that artless virtue both threat and promise. Bob was headed squarely for such a life, and I saw the ease of mind he carried into it, and I worried for that dangerous innocence.

A fat squirrel braved the dark clearing to look me over. Its tail was magnificent, textured gray and silver, a feathered curve, and as it stood on hindquarters I saw a patch of pink belly. I whistled, very softly, and the squirrel's eyes widened and held a second before it shot back into the brush. Then I heard Bob's step on the trail. He offered a very poor imitation of an owl from about twenty yards out.

"That was the worst owl I've ever heard," I said.

Bob's good laugh came back to me through the trees. "Would you care to get out of here, get that deer to the butcher?"

I stood, brushing off my pants. "Most definitely," I said.

Another crunching of leaves and Bob was at my shoulder. "We just walked past our cutoff. Too much talking or something."

"Worrying so hard about missing the trail we didn't see it," I said.

"I guess," Bob said. "It's no more than sixty yards back, maybe less. I got it marked."

Moonlight sheltered into the trees. Bob slung his rifle and we picked up the deer. I watched his strong back, wider across than mine, as he muscled his end of the carry-pole toward our trail, and felt the balanced light in our affinity, a quiet and shadowed heat. My anxiety eased as we walked, and dispersed in my gratitude for the small deliverance in moving toward what I knew.

the presence of God or faith or the manifest unknown that existed beyond us, without us, akin in soul and conviction to the widening palm of the morning sky, the frame of high tattered cloud I saw through the window in my door. I stood then and walked to the trailer's one closet to bring out a shoebox from under the folded haversack Bob and I used when we went hunting or camping. I took the box back to the kitchen counter and sifted through the old collection of letters from Riva, fragments of lyrics scratched on napkins and ragged bits of notepaper, and found the clipping. The only review the Still Creek Boys ever received, in a Nashville trade tabloid.

The clipping was in an envelope. I opened it carefully, creases grained into brittle newsprint. I once counted the words in the review, riding along some lost highway in the Chrysler. Sixty-four words.

The date at the top of the page was May 17, 1953. The column was called "New Release Roundup," with our mention halfway down the page. *A standout from Castle Records is Sapper Reeves and his trio, a superbly talented ensemble offering a fine collection of originals penned by Reeves along with heartfelt versions of two mountain traditionals. "Miranda" and "Over the Next Hill" in particular bear the hallmarks of songs that will stand the test of time. Reeves's stunning banjo dexterity and haunting vocals lead the way. Highly recommended.*

I folded the clipping away and replaced the lid on the box. A car turned into the trailer park, crunching gravel in the drive as it passed. I uncapped the Jack Daniel's and poured two inches into a jelly glass.

Lifting the glass, I paused, then placed it back on the

2

I PLAYED the Gibson Mastertone that Estin had given me, alone in the trailer, following the instrument's strength and the elegant persuasion in its voice. The banjo carried my hand rather than simply accepting it, spacious and fluid. I was up and dressed for work and needed to go but could not move, sitting on the sofa with the banjo and working into the melody with a nearly secretive care. I played "Miranda," whispering the lyrics to let the song rise in my mind and the silence of the morning.

I sat with the first hours of daylight, the banjo resting on the sofa beside me. I had wanted so much, yet never more than what I believed to be right and proper, and as the years passed I had drawn away into the spaces of that belief, without rectification, perhaps; into belief that had little to do with anything beyond the vagaries of mind and desire. I could posit the wisdom of balance in an unfolding universe, counter and looked down at it a moment before I turned to pour the contents into the sink.

I was late to work that morning for the first time since Ben Sedge hired me. I came in by the alley door, embarrassed, lied to Ben about my truck being slow to start.

3

ON A morning after I played with my pickup band of high school boys at a small college near Maxwell, a guitarist I had never met called me at the hardware store, asking if I might join him on a regular basis at Petrie's Bar and Grill, a roadhouse west of Maxwell on Route 50. It was to be just the two of us, he explained, an informal duo playing primarily for fun, although the roadhouse owner promised a small paycheck in exchange for a regular commitment on Wednesday and Saturday nights. I stood behind the counter with the phone to my ear, customers milling around the store, browsing in the aisles, beyond them the pearled light of midwinter filling the store window and the street. *Well,* I heard myself saying, *sounds interesting, let's give it a try.*

We met to rehearse. My new partner was an earnest history teacher at Maxwell High, a more than passable musician with an abiding interest in country music. The old songs pressed forward with a presence and casual grace that both surprised and reassured me, and I extended or rewrote verses for several of the tunes, added variations, improvised new breaks and bridges when I found I had forgotten the ones I played night after night in the years on the road. We played what we liked at Petrie's, slow and fast, new or old, and it was a good and gentle thing to be playing that way again, in a quiet taproom on a country road with a scatter of people who smiled and nodded and sometimes stood to dance. I played without expectation or received image, only the rise and fall of the music itself, the restrained integrity of the songs, lives of their own.

The arrangement at Petrie's was three months along when I looked out at the patrons on a Wednesday night and saw Riva sitting alone at a table near the back. She lifted her hand in a gentle wave. I nodded in return.

At the break I walked back to the table. Riva did not move, smiling slightly, watching my approach.

"Can I join you for a few minutes?" I asked.

She gestured at the empty chair across the table. I sat, asking how she heard I was playing at Petrie's.

"Bobby, of course," she said. "You think your son would let this go by and not tell me? He loves to listen to you, anyway."

"He does? He's never told me."

"Probably never will, either. He's not always very forthcoming."

I smiled. "Inherited from me?"

"I don't know. Can a person pass on qualities like that?"

"I'm not sure," I said. "I hope not. I wouldn't want to be blamed for anything."

Riva looked toward the little stage, a platform two feet above the floor. "How's it feel?"

I turned in the same direction: the banjo and guitar stood in their racks under muted light. "Good," I said. "I'll admit it's pretty good."

"You sound . . ." Riva paused and turned back to me. "You sound wonderful. Your voice is even better. It's rougher and wiser, but I think that's because you drink too much."

I broke eye contact, pushed the top of my tongue against my teeth. "I'm working on that," I said.

"Well," Riva said, "that's good to hear."

"Estin was up," I said quickly.

Riva nodded. "Bob told me that too. Guess he stopped by your place and you two were in there playing together?"

"That we were," I said. "We've been doing more of that in the last year or so."

"Wish you'd invite me over to listen sometime. I'd be a very willing audience of one."

"Okay," I said, "I think we could do that. Estin asks about you every time I talk to him anyway. I imagine he'd love to see you."

"He's doing well?"

"I think so, yes," I said. "Got a pretty good little business going down there in Memphis."

Riva leaned forward in her chair. "Now all you need is Leonard."

I laughed. "I'm too old for Leonard James."

"You ever hear from him?"

"Not really. Now and then. Postcard from time to time. He phoned me in the middle of the night a couple years ago. Just like Leonard."

"He still out in Las Vegas?"

"Far as I know. Plays in Elvis Presley's band at one of the hotels. He invited me out."

"You should go," Riva said.

"Well," I said. "I don't think so."

Riva leaned away from me, pulled her hands into her lap. I asked how things were going for her at the produce market where she had worked for the past several years.

"Very good," she said. "Matter of fact, it couldn't be better. I'm half owner."

"Half owner?"

Riva mocked my surprise, imitating my expression and saying, "Yes sir, half owner."

"That's . . . well, that's great. I just . . . You *bought* a share?"

"It took years to save the money, Sapper. Yes, I bought it. Nobody gets rich selling produce, but it's steady. And we're expanding."

She went on to talk about her stake in the crossroads fruit and vegetable stand, which prospered all summer and most of the winter, her voice gathering around her perseverance, now resonant with the life of its telling, a thing I welcomed for years: Riva talking to me, simply talking, her voice low and warm, as much a part of my loving her as anything else between us. I watched her and listened and she stopped and looked at the table. She asked if I knew about Bob's decision.

"Decision?"

"About the Marines."

"What about the Marines?"

"He's joining."

I was brought up short, startled. "He's joining the Marines?"

"I told him to talk to you about it," Riva said. "But I figured he hadn't. Thought I better force the issue."

"He wants to be a police officer," I said. "He's wanted to be a cop since he was a little guy."

"And he still does, I think. But he's also offered me the idea that a stint in the military will help him in terms of a career in law enforcement." Riva shifted her gaze around the room. "And there's the Vietnam thing."

"What do you mean?"

She sighed. "He's in what I think you might call a patriotic fervor. You know Bobby. This sort of thing appeals to him."

"I wouldn't think getting killed would appeal to anybody. Besides, that's a two-bit war. The president himself doesn't have a goddamn clue what's going on over there."

Riva looked directly at me. "He's a teenage boy, Sapper. He stands up every morning in school to pledge allegiance to the flag. He's influenced by all kinds of things. Coaches, teachers —"

"None of whom are joining the Marines."

Riva studied me. "And Bobby is who he is on top of that. The kind of boy he is."

I blinked at Riva, and swallowed. I was abruptly beyond words, pressed beyond conversation, knowing she was right. After a moment I said I should have a talk with Bob.

"You should, of course," Riva said. "He certainly needs to discuss this with you. But I think his mind is made up. Besides, there's the draft. A boy like him could end up with no choice at all."

"So is that why you came tonight? To tell me about Bob?"

"Partly. But I could have called you about Bobby."

"You could have," I said.

"I wanted to hear you play, Sapper. It's been a long time."

I took a breath, looking at her. "Yes," I said. "It has been. A long time."

"Well, then," she said, "play some more for me."

"Any special requests?"

Riva brought her hands back into view, folded them, and rested them on the table. "Just play for me, Sapper."

While I was driving away from Petrie's that night, it started to rain. A slick of two-lane blacktop disappeared beneath my truck, and I traveled along a berm of falling water, everything in fragile motion at the heart of the world, the full-throated rake of thunder and tremble of my own lagging mind. I was tired — ten hours at the hardware store and three more on the little stage at Petrie's — and did not steer so much as sense the natural magnetism of the highway, that borne-away flank of ragged trust. There were names of towns I recalled from the days on the road with the band, so accurate and dreamlike it seemed they could not exist in a daylight world: Lightburn, Century, Angel, signs flickering past rain-smeared windows, lost forever unless you happened to be looking at the moment of passage.

I reached the Maxwell city limit, turned left onto Route 19, slowed as I came into town. I had not intended or anticipated going anywhere other than my trailer, but I turned right on Davis and left onto Delmartin, slowed and pulled to a stop across the street from Riva's house, cut the engine. The house was dark except for the single lamp in the living room window. She might be awake.

She might be sitting beside the lamp, I thought, reading a magazine. Watching television, or simply sitting in the chair and thinking without inclination to interruption, Bob asleep in his room, the rest of the house dark. Or she might not be there at all, the lamp forgotten, left to bleed light into an empty room.

My hands in front of me on the wheel. Vein and tendon rising in matrix and pattern, crossing each other under the shadow of skin. I realized she might not welcome me, arriving on impulse and uninvited like some accidental veteran of best intentions and ignorant love. Returning without a story to tell. I looked again at the house and stepped down out of the truck to walk across the wet street. I tapped gently on the door.

In a moment she opened. I looked at her from the porch. The back of my shirt was damp from rain.

"Sapper," she said.

"Riva."

"It's late."

"I apologize about the hour," I said. "I wonder if I might come in? I thought perhaps we could talk."

She said nothing for a moment, watching my face, and stepped aside in the doorway. "You're getting wet out there," she said.

Spring 1968

1

BOB HAD been in the Marine Corps for nearly a year when the man named Alan Bernstein came to visit. I stood on the porch of the house on Delmartin Street and waited as the long tan Cadillac pulled to a stop. A young woman dressed as if she wanted to match the car — shades of copper and beige, heavy gold jewelry, hair the color of sand — got out on the passenger side. Bernstein stepped out from behind the wheel: perhaps thirty-five years old, a wild spray of black hair on either side of his head, bald on top. The suit was a charcoal pinstripe, double-breasted. He waved at me from the car, as if we were old friends.

Bernstein had called a few days earlier, identifying himself as a concert promoter, asking if he might visit. He wanted to discuss my appearance at a concert in New York, he said, at Carnegie Hall. He told me he wanted to make his proposal face-to-face, *the best thing to do,* he told me, *out of respect for your reputation.*

"Mr. Bernstein," I said as he walked toward the porch. He pumped my hand, looking over my shoulder at the open front door. He nudged his head toward the young woman behind him, introducing her only as his assistant. She moved toward me and took my hand but did not shake it, simply held it and looked carefully into my eyes and told me how deeply excited she was to meet me. Bernstein cleared his throat.

I led them into the kitchen and offered coffee.

"I'd love some," the woman said.

I pulled out chairs around the table; Bernstein and his assistant sat. I brought cups and saucers down from the cabinet over the stove and set them out with spoons and a cream pitcher and sugar bowl. Bernstein looked around, a cursory study, then told me that Maxwell was certainly a damn long way from New York.

"That last hundred miles seemed to go on forever," he said, looking more to his assistant than to me.

I put the water on to boil. "So," I said. "You're putting together a concert?"

"Not just any concert, either," Bernstein said, relieved to move directly to business, his voice suddenly louder, more affable. He brought his eyebrows together, glaring at me. "Mr. Reeves, we're here to invite you to play, as an honored guest, in a major concert in New York City. A retrospective of country music. The best this kind of music has to offer. The first such event of its kind."

He paused, looking at me. His assistant smiled and quietly added that they expected this concert to make musical history.

"Cultural history," Bernstein emphasized.

I nodded, pausing a moment before I asked if either of them took cream or sugar.

Bernstein wanted his coffee black. I looked at his assistant; she said cream would be fine with her. "I don't believe I caught your name," I said.

She blinked, confused, glancing quickly at Bernstein before saying, "Helen. Helen Riggs."

Bernstein carried on, warming to his mission. "Making history is exactly how I see it, Mr. Reeves. I'm bringing together the greatest names in country music for a once-in-a-lifetime show. The innovators, the great stylists. The originals. And we'll have some of the best of the newer generation, too. There'll be a concert album, possibly a two-record set. A royalty arrangement on that, of course."

I nodded again and held an attentive pose. I was not immediately sure how to respond, or whether I should respond at all.

"I've got commitments from Tammy Wynette, from George Jones and Bill Monroe, Johnny Cash, Willie Nelson. To name a few. Several people mentioned you. Tammy actually told me the roster is incomplete until you're on it. And I completely agree."

"Well," I said. "Sounds like it'll be quite a show."

"We're negotiating a concert film, too. I think I mentioned that this kind of concert has never been done before."

I drew a breath and let it go slowly. "You a country-music fan, Mr. Bernstein?"

"Absolutely, most definitely." He spread his hands and lifted his head. "Sure, you'd never think it, right? A kid from Long Island? The son of an accountant? I guess you could call it an acquired taste. A few years back I went to one of those fiddlers' conventions, and you know, I was hooked."

"Any favorite musicians? Songs you like in particular?"

"I'll tell you one thing," Bernstein said. "*You're* one of my favorites." He looked at Helen Riggs. "We were just talking about that on the way down, weren't we? How I love the music of Sapper Reeves?"

Helen Riggs beamed at me.

I said it was hard to find much of my music.

"Come on," Bernstein said, "it's out there. If you love this music, it's there. And when they reissued that original album of yours . . . well, that record's hooked a lot more people than you might think. I've heard talk about how young musicians have passed that album around, hand to hand. I mean, the reissue of a benchmark album that's been lost for a decade? Christ, look at what that did for Robert Johnson. Do you realize what kind of . . . what's that word you used, Helen?"

"Cachet," Helen said.

"There you go," Bernstein said. "And then having your songs recorded by other artists in the last few years hasn't hurt any. Look, Mr. Reeves, this is why we want you at Carnegie Hall. In a nutshell. It's your *influence* we're talking about here. It's huge."

I looked toward the window. The crests of the oaks were in bud against the light. The kettle sang, and I turned to pour the water.

"And I'll tell you something, Mr. Reeves," Bernstein said. "Bringing you in on this would be a coup. You know what I'm saying?"

I poured the first cup of steaming water over the coffee grounds as Bernstein leaned toward Helen Riggs and said, "Can you imagine the effect this guy will have, walking out on that stage? It'll be nearly *mystical.*"

I poured the second cup.

Helen stood and came around the table, saying that she

would finish the coffee, I should sit and relax. "Mr. Reeves," she said, "what Al's trying to say is simply this: you're a legend. You're one of those musicians who pointed the way. So much of what we have now is because of the markers you laid down years ago. There's a whole new generation of listeners out there who need to hear from you."

"Beautifully put," Bernstein said from his seat, clapping his hands. "Beautifully put."

I gave the coffee over to Helen Riggs and took the chair opposite Bernstein. She stepped around, filling our cups. "You know," Bernstein said, "I really think you should give this concert serious consideration."

"I *am* giving it serious consideration," I said. "Why would you think I'm not?"

"I don't know. You're . . . quiet, I guess. I thought you'd be shouting from the rooftops."

"I may yet," I said. "How's the coffee?"

Bernstein looked steadily across at me, waiting a moment, assessing. "I can get into the business details, if that's what you need — performance fees, royalty structure, back-end residuals. If that's what you want to hear right now."

"Go ahead," I said.

"You have an agent?"

I sipped coffee, replaced the cup on the saucer. "No sir," I said, "I don't."

"Bad idea," Bernstein said. "I should refer you to some people." He grimaced. "I refer you and they take me to the cleaners." The grimace fell away, and he shrugged. "Well, nature of the business." He talked on, a staccato chatter, making the pitch, his voice closing over contractual specifics, and I smelled the waning afternoon through the open window, a gentle premonition of rain. Helen Riggs slipped quietly away from the table as Bernstein lectured, looking at the pictures Riva had arranged on shelving along one wall of the kitchen: a family portrait from the late 1950s; Bob hefting his trophy at the state wrestling championships; a picture of me in performance, lit from below, standing close to a microphone in wide dark space; a lustrous oval of Riva, taken not long after she graduated from high school. Bernstein finished and asked me how it all sounded.

Helen Riggs turned to find me looking at her. "Is this Mrs. Reeves?" she asked, pointing at the oval.

"It is," I said.

"Not home today?"

"She's working," I said. "She's part owner of a business here in town."

Helen asked about the picture of me.

"World's Original Jamboree," I said. "Wheeling, West Virginia. Nineteen fifty."

Bernstein craned his neck to look. "The *Jamboree?* I read about that show. One of the big players of its time?"

I gazed at the photograph. "So I was told," I said.

Helen smiled and moved back to the table.

Bernstein asked me again how his deal sounded. I looked at him. "Pretty good," I said.

"Just pretty good?"

"It's fine," I said. "Mr. Bernstein, I'm very grateful that you came down here to speak personally with me about this. I would be happy to appear in your concert. Very happy."

Bernstein clapped his hands together again, as if he were applauding himself.

"One condition," I said.

"What's that?"

"I play with my band. The Still Creek Boys."

Bernstein studied me. "You're kidding. You can bring together the original band? The same guys who played with you on that record?"

"The same guys," I said.

Bernstein nodded vigorously. "You got it," he said.

2

I SAW Alan Bernstein and Helen Riggs to the door, watched them drive away, and went back into the kitchen. It was close to five; Riva would not be home for another two hours. I toasted a slice of bread and carried it and my unfinished coffee to the back porch and sat.

The yard framed in silence, the particular haunt and given territory of my son and the neighborhood's children, all gone into the beginnings of lives. Early clumps of bluegrass struggling up. The sky deepening to the west, an occasional tatter of cloud.

I determined to wait a day or two before phoning Estin, to settle my thoughts and the blatant impulse to race toward Bernstein's offer as if it would at last change my life. I told myself it was good to hold a measured distance, standing between fright and elation — or simply so removed from either that I could not accurately sense my own mind. Or in a swale of both, fear and euphoria hunkered down on uncertain ground.

Carnegie Hall: no picture came to mind. I offered myself an image of a stage, broad and uncluttered as an open field, and beyond the field the rows of dark and empty seats, aisles and balconies, brocade curtains, a windswept mahogany light. At first an eerie vacancy, then they are there: the hundreds, the faces lined into the tiered seats, shapes and glints and patches of luminous color melting into darkness at the back of the room.

I finished the toast and coffee and went inside to turn on the television for the six o'clock news. Every night there was news of Vietnam and I watched, wanting to know as much as I could about the war, how it had come to pass and might end, toying with the possibility of hearing something about Bob's unit, the random hope of catching sight of him in the blurred clumps of soldiers I saw hanging in the frame behind the newscasters or crossing through the shots, mounting a bridge, approaching the camera along a yellow dirt road.

I consulted an atlas at the Maxwell Public Library, looking for Vietnam. I located the edge of topography on page 136, a child's arm reaching south into ocean. Bob wrote every few weeks from that page with nothing much to say. Where he was, where he might be going next if he knew, place names I could not pronounce. I sat at the kitchen table with the soft blue onionskin his letters were written on, reading aloud to Riva: *Dak To, Can Tho, Tan Son Nhut. I love you both, see you soon.*

I stared at the television: a state senator embezzled thousands from a miners' welfare fund, the governor lacked popular support for a tax reform package, a car crash near Weston claimed the lives of two. Three commercials. The broadcaster returned with a map of Vietnam projected behind his head, saying that U.S. Marines had retreated the day before from the mountains south of the demilitarized zone in the face of a heavy assault from the North Vietnamese Army. Civilians were being evacuated from the area. I watched the television screen, working to bring Bob into the disparate scraps of information I heard, thinking every night I might catch a glimpse. And what would he look like, I asked myself, in a flickering ten-second fade on the evening news, the low-voltage arc of a newsman's hand-held camera, and there, *there:* fatigued, yes, most certainly that. The hint of his old grin but his mouth now turned against itself, if only slightly; the shadow of something buried, behind his eyes but still alive there, a tactile essence. I wanted to see him, if only once, to tell Riva *The kid made the news, looks like he's all right,* and I was afraid to see him in the same drawn breath, afraid for what I might notice, the pulse of some fingered and reaching fear, the soft and distant turbulence of an honest regret. I did not insult my son by imagining that we could share a similar level of fear, but when I reached toward him from my mind the anguish was so palpable it vibrated. I watched, and waited, and never saw him, his face always the one I created, Lance Corporal Bob Reeves smeared with jungle mud, dripping from days of rain, his rifle slung and helmet cocked back on his forehead and looking, for a single moment, directly into the camera.

3

RIVA OPENED the front door shortly after seven; I heard her step in and close the door, move into the kitchen to put something on the table. Then her voice behind me in the doorway. "Sapper? Are you okay?"

"Fine," I said. "Waiting for you."

She pushed the door open and came onto the porch, sat in the chair beside me. "Did the man from New York make it in?"

"Oh yes," I said, "that he did."

"And?"

"It sounds good," I said. "More than good, actually. Terrific. Marvelous."

"Sapper." Riva sat forward in the chair. "That's wonderful. What does he have in mind? What sort of concert is it?"

"It's a collection, basically."

"A collection?"

"A string of performers. Remarkable group of people, in fact. He wants to present the history of the music through its artists, I think, my generation, the current one. The old and the new." I paused, looking out toward the alley. "I didn't know what to say to him."

"I gather you accepted the offer?"

"Oh yes, definitely. But he went on about my reputation, what I stand for, that sort of thing. I felt . . . I don't know. Frightened, for lack of a better word."

Riva reached her hand across and touched my arm. "You gave up on this sort of thing happening."

"I was . . . prepared for the possibility that I would finish my life on two nights a week at Petrie's. The occasional college folk festival. Yes."

"But not prepared for the possibility that you would go to Carnegie Hall and play in the company you belong in."

I gave a short laugh. "No," I said, "not prepared for that. It's as if I dreamed it, Riva. As if I woke up and told you about a funny dream I had, where a man drives down from New York, all the way to Maxwell, West Virginia, with an outlandish idea."

"But this is no dream. You'll be there."

"And Estin and Leonard. I'm taking them along. It's fitting."

Riva smiled in the half-light. "You call either of them yet?"

"I'll wait a bit on that. Wanted to hold the news close for a couple days. Just you and me. Savor it, I guess."

We sat then in the ticking silence of dusk, paling light still alive above the rooftops, the sky burnished and on the ground our hedgerow at the back of the yard gone to black, a squared ledge of shadow along the alley. A few dark birds circled, scissoring the air to drop suddenly out of flight, into the boughs of our neighbor's sycamore. Riva asked if I had watched the news.

"Nothing much," I said. "Starts to sound the same, night after night."

"I know. Assaults, retreats. No end in sight."

"So," I said. "More of that today."

"Any mail?"

"Well," I said, "nothing from Bobby."

Riva said something about needing to get to her flower beds, her voice nearly a whisper, a remote murmur. Then, louder, "It's fine news, this concert. You'll be at your best, Sapper. All of you will."

"I think that we will be, Riva. I know we will be."

Riva stood, asking if I had eaten anything yet.

"Slice of toast. Some coffee."

Riva said it seemed to her an excellent night to go out, drive down to Clarksburg for some Italian food. "How does that sound?"

"Very good," I said. "Very good indeed."

We made love that night, as comfortable in each other's bodies as ever, the lot of fortune still tuned in our movements: a careful searching, fingertips to palms, a refined grace unwinding into what becomes fated, the pure weight of the moment driving us together on a road we had always traveled, arching into the darkness, reaching for it and the blessing of a night that slid away into dreams I cannot recall and it was morning, an ethereal light sweeping against the shuttered windows as I awoke.

Riva moved closer under the blankets, her body warm and folded against my side. She asked if it was time to get up, murmuring the question into my neck.

"Probably," I said, turning to hold her, listening to the

quiet house. All through the years of his boyhood Bob was an early riser, lights on, radio on, water running, toilet flushing, a boy humming to himself in front of the mirror. Always ready for the day. When Bob was with me on weekends, I would shuffle into the trailer's tiny bathroom to find him whistling, slicking his brown hair into place, giving me a gentle punch on the shoulder.

I slipped away from Riva and out of bed to pull on my bathrobe, went to the kitchen to put water on for coffee.

III

Summer 1968

1

THE TELEGRAM was delivered at the hardware store. A young man I did not know handed the envelope across the counter and thrust a clipboard toward me, saying he needed a signature to verify delivery. I signed in the numbered box he pointed at.

I put the envelope aside and finished ringing up a sale. Then I turned away from the register and picked up the envelope and drew my thumb under the flap to open it. I was aware of Ben Sedge several feet away, watching me from where he crouched in front of a shelf.

I drew out the piece of paper and unfolded it and read the message. THE SECRETARY OF THE NAVY HAS ASKED ME TO EXPRESS HIS DEEP REGRET THAT YOUR SON LANCE CORPORAL ROBERT L. REEVES WOUNDED IN ACTION 21 APRIL 1968 ON COMBAT OPERATION WHEN HIT BY HOSTILE GRENADE FRAGMENTS FURTHER INFORMATION

TO FOLLOW. THIS CONFIRMS PERSONAL NOTIFICATION MADE BY A REPRESENTATIVE OF THE SECRETARY OF THE NAVY. BENNETT O. GREENE, MAJOR GENERAL USMC, ADJUTANT GENERAL.

I read the telegram a second time and looked up from the page at Ben. He asked if everything was okay. I walked the few steps between us and handed him the telegram.

He read and handed it back and looked away. He said I had better go on and see Riva. He was in the middle of stacking boxes of lawn fertilizer but made no move to continue his work. I waited a moment before I turned and walked out of the store.

Sitting behind the wheel in my truck, I read the telegram a third time. *Hostile grenade fragments.* What did that mean? A nick? A graze? Blown past recognition? Anger bloomed in me then, an accelerating resentment filling my throat and chest, pained and ravenous. I tossed the telegram onto the seat and drove for Riva.

She sat with the telegram on the sofa, lips pressed tightly, face white and empty as she read the message through.

She read it once standing on the gravel parking lot of her produce market, again on the drive home as she sat beside me. Now she folded the message and slipped it into the envelope and placed the envelope on her lap. Her hands fell forward against her thighs. She looked up at me and quickly her eyes tracked away, to the floor. I sat down next to her and held her, and she turned her face toward me to weep quietly against my chest.

After a time I said that I needed to walk. She asked if she should come with me and I said no, I needed an hour or so, on my feet and moving, outside.

2

I WALKED away from Delmartin, across Main Street, hearing people greet me. I cannot recall if I returned the greetings; probably not. I turned up the Grand Street hill and climbed, past the ornate houses of our two lawyers and the doctor and the judge, past the stone mansion owned by a coal operator, up and beyond the houses and past the end of the brick pavement and out to the ridge that overlooked the town, to the point where I gazed down on the clutter of buildings and thin web of streets in a dirty spring drizzle. A ragged finger of smoke worked into the overcast from the garbage fires backed against Tanner's Hill across the river, and I stood beside a small hickory tree. I did not tell myself I couldn't believe it: that's what people always say, *I just couldn't believe it,* believing having so little to do with the fate of my son or anything else, all the sanctioned alibis of belief brought to bear — conviction, intuition, splintering faith —

none of it so true as a sheet of canary paper from the Department of Defense, nothing so unalterable, so rigidly etched wherever I turned. Bob was hurt, perhaps dead, in another universe, in some tired and unforgiving and inevitable second patched into all the pictures I saw each night on the news, the other world we were given: a belt of bullets ticking through a machine gun and the gunner's teeth locked closed as his face and arms jerked with the gun's hysterical recoil; naked children running toward the camera, sobbing as a village gushed flame behind them.

Fear washed into me then, as sudden as an animal's, surging and different from anything I knew or remembered, a rabid dismay that left me aghast and unbalanced by its power. Breath spiraled out of control and the sky turned on its pivot. I reached for the water-slick bark of the hickory for purchase, missed, and slipped to nearly fall, took hold of a branch and steadied. I was in flood, my heart punching under my ribs, and the rain came harder, soaking my hair and shirt in seconds, dripping from my nose and chin and for a moment thundering around me, pelting the ground to mud.

I held to the tree and turned my face to the sky and accepted the torrent, the roar of water, and the rain eased then, as swiftly as it had come, its fresh cold calming, calling back a measure of balance. I turned to the town spread below me to find church spires rising in mist and the courthouse's big shoulders and the river's valley cut. The Water Street railroad bridge stood out over the river; Route 19 threaded into the hills, toward the smeared horizon.

I pushed water out of my hair and away from my eyes. Far below, due east, the abandoned paper mill and its trash-littered roof crouched below the railroad tracks. Water Street curved away from the plant's high fence to cross Delmartin and Main and slope south. Across the valley the hills lifted into a soft green wilderness, time going on forever, the open dream of the land.

3

THE SERGEANT who took my call at the Pentagon made no show of consolation. His clipped voice was flat and uninvolved.

"Sir," he said, "that information is unavailable at this time."

"I got a telegram earlier today," I said, "so it's not entirely unavailable."

"That's only the advance word, sir. Comprehensive data from a combat theater can be a long time coming. Depending on the location of our forces at the time of engagement, the nature of your son's wound, the evac destination. There's a number of variables. I'm sure you understand."

"No," I said, "I don't think I do."

"Perhaps not, sir."

"Listen, I want to know what's happened to my son. I have a right to know." This brought no response from the sergeant. "And somewhere in that organization," I continued, "is someone who knows or can find out."

"I doubt that, sir. What was the date of casualty again?"

I struggled against shouting. "April twenty-first," I said.

"Well, sir, there you are. Less than ten days ago. Records don't routinely reach stateside for up to three weeks post-injury. At that time we'll have a full status report."

"Three weeks?"

"Yes, sir. As a rule. Sometimes longer."

"This is unbelievable," I said. My voice dropped to a hoarse whisper.

"Not at all, sir. It's a big war. And a long way off."

"Do you have a supervisor, sergeant?"

"That would be Captain Greider, sir."

"Put him on the phone."

"Sir, I'm afraid the captain is at lunch."

"Jesus," I whispered.

"Sir?"

"Leave the captain a message. Can you do that much?"

"Of course."

"Tell him the parents of Lance Corporal Robert Reeves need word on their son. You have his service number, I gave that to you."

"Yes, sir."

"Tell him we need word."

"I'll leave this note on his desk, sir. Thank you for calling."

4

"NO, WE HAVE no information on that sort of thing, Mr. Reeves." A young woman's voice, full-timbered and practiced. "The senator doesn't receive lists or anything like that."

She paused. I said nothing, uncertain what I could ask next.

"It certainly is very hard news," she continued. "I'm so sorry. I'm certain the senator would share in that."

I took a breath and asked if there was anything at all that could be done.

"As I mentioned, Mr. Reeves, we're not routinely notified. I can imagine you and your wife are very concerned."

I swallowed and said, "You're telling me there's absolutely nothing you can do? There's no access to information that I don't have? A United States senator can't at least make an inquiry?"

"There's the Public Affairs Office at the Pentagon. Perhaps they could help."

"I've been there already. And no, they couldn't help. At all."

"I see. I'm sorry."

"They said it could be as long as a month before we hear."

"Tell you what, Mr. Reeves. I'll enter a query from this office. Who did you talk to at the Pentagon?"

I gave her the name and number.

"I'll ask them to expedite this. But I doubt the request coming from this office will make much difference. There's a lot of soldiers in Vietnam. They're probably overwhelmed at the Pentagon."

I suddenly felt an urgency to be free of the conversation's uselessness, clear of the unctuous voice and the whine of distant wind echoing on the wire. The young woman started to speak and I interrupted. "Just tell them we're waiting," I said, and hung up.

5

ARLON GATES had moved on from a stint as Maxwell's town manager to a job working for the governor out of a storefront office in Clarksburg. He was standing at a cabinet when I walked in, sifting through files in an open drawer. He turned at the sound of the door and stared when he saw me.

"Jesus H. Christ. Is that you, Sapper?"

I stopped at the reception counter. "It's me, Arlon. How are you?"

He shoved the drawer closed and marched toward me with an extended hand. "Long time, Sapper. Too long."

"Too long," I said.

"You doing all right? Still working at the hardware store?"

"Still there."

"That's good. You were the best thing to happen to that damn place. Ben Sedge is always in such a terrible mood. Born with a chip on his shoulder. Nobody wants to deal with him."

"Is there a place we can talk, Arlon?"

He paused, then nodded. "Sure, of course. My office is right back there."

He led me to a partitioned room built into a corner, waist-high windows on three sides. He stepped in, pointing at a chair in front of his desk. He dropped into his own chair and swiveled a half-turn to face me. "What's on your mind, old buddy?"

I told him about the telegram.

He listened until I finished describing my telephone encounters with both the Pentagon and a senator's secretary. "Arlon, it's been eleven days . . ." I stopped, looked to the side, forced my teeth together. I felt as if I might lose control.

"Riva and you are about out of your minds, I guess."

I simply nodded.

He leaned forward on his elbows and pushed a hand over his face, exhaled heavily. "Bobby. Christ, I didn't know he was even old enough to be in the service."

"Time gets by, Arlon."

"I guess it does, at that."

"Can you help me? All Riva and I want is some news. What his condition is. Where he is. If he's alive."

"Well," Arlon said, "you know I'll absolutely do my best. I'll see if I can throw any weight around."

I pulled a pad closer and wrote my phone number on it and pressed it across the desk. "Anytime," I said. "Any news you get. Anything at all."

Arlon drew a sheet of typing paper from a tray and copied my phone number along the top of the page. "Better let me have some details," he said. "You have the telegram with you?"

I gave it to him. He culled out the notification date, the name of Bennett Greene, asked for Bob's service number and the precise unit he served with. "Let's see what I come up with," he said.

We walked together from his office toward the front door. Arlon asked if I still played the banjo. There was a flicker of trepidation in his voice.

I paused at the door. "You don't have to be afraid to ask, Arlon."

He shrugged. "Well, I know how tough it was, trying to keep the band together, cobble together a living and all. But Christ, Sapper, you were something to hear, I'm telling you."

"I still play," I said.

Arlon offered a companionable pat on the shoulder. "Hey, that's great, old buddy. That's terrific. Let me know where I can come and hear you."

"Any news you come up with about Bob," I said. "Riva and I would be very grateful."

"Absolutely. I'll be on top of this right away. This afternoon."

6

RIVA AND I went to our jobs, worked the days through, came home to mark silent company. We started conversations that withered, ate quietly, turned on the television, turned it off again.

On Sunday — the second Sunday after receiving the telegram — Riva worked in her flower beds. From where I sat on the back porch I heard the rasp of her trowel punching into dry soil along the side of the house. I sat in a wicker chair with my banjo, moving notes around the scale, some random fragments of melody. I looked across the square of grass, over the alley, out to the sky opening beyond the town. I had practiced the banjo on the back porch on Waterhill Ridge, looking into the sky in the same way. That was a hospitable sky until after my father died; then it was muted, larger than it had ever been, nebulous but I liked to believe wise, in some way a repository of wisdom that was at least gentle, at least that much. I practiced from that vantage, note for note, chord for labored chord. It was on the porch that I first told my mother about a rough plan to make my living as a musician.

She was snapping pole beans into a colander and smiled quietly over her work. She did not reject the idea out of hand, but suggested it was not a particularly likely option.

Not that you couldn't do it, son, she said.

What, then, I asked her.

She paused, looking up and out across the valley. I guess it's who we are. Where we are.

I could try, I told her.

She glanced at me and back to her beans. That you could, she said. That you could.

I turned to the valley after that conversation: a storm was building under the clouds, falling toward the wooded faces below. Clouds the color of earth, rising to move headlong across the distances like runaway horses. I watched the rain come toward me forever.

Two o'clock in the morning. I sat alone at the kitchen table, in the dark. It no longer mattered what I thought I knew, or might have learned, or remembered, or how I passed my days: now the earth with its tilt and spin in what I could only assume was a volatile emptiness seemed the only inalienable fact there was. My breath struck a chord against the span of night so faint as to be nearly inaudible, and yet without that touch of sound — the knowledge of its existence — the night's clocking distance threatened to drown me. I felt darkness rising to meet my exhaustion, the search and pull of my mind unwinding. The shapes in the room hovered, the hulk of the humming refrigerator, the stovetop's patina, the slow and mired poverty of vision in that crumbling hour.

"Sapper?"

I looked up, startled: Riva in the kitchen doorway, in her nightgown.

"Sapper, this is no good. Come to bed."

"Couldn't sleep," I said. "Didn't want to wake you."

She came to the table and sat down. "I wasn't sleeping too well myself." She put her hand over mine. "I bet we get some news real soon," she said softly. After another moment she said, "Why don't you come back to bed."

I studied the back of her hand, its shape and harbored grace. A train whistle sang from the Water Street bridge. "You go ahead," I said. "I'll be right along."

7

ARLON GATES guided his car to the curb and parked. Riva and I stood on the porch, waiting.

He came up the walk, necktie pulled loose and slightly askew. He shook my hand, kissed Riva on the cheek, and followed us inside to take a chair in the living room. Riva and I sat together on the sofa.

"Bobby's okay," Arlon said immediately. "He's hurt, but he'll make it."

"Hurt," Riva said. "What kind of hurt?"

Arlon's tongue traced his lower lip.

"Where'd you get the information?" I asked.

"Same places you tried and couldn't get the time of day, Sapper. I managed to get the governor's office involved, and we got a direct phone line opened up to Vietnam. Took a few hours and some shouting to put that in place, but we got it done."

"What kind of hurt?" Riva asked again.

Arlon studied us both, then looked toward his knees. I could see him gathering himself for whatever it was he had come to say. Then he looked up again and moved firmly ahead. "Bob's lost his right hand. And his right eye."

A wordless sound came from me then, involuntary, a guttural cough.

Riva sat unmoving. She said nothing. I could hear her breathing, measured and stolid.

I saw Arlon swallow heavily, his throat contracting. "The way I heard it was Bobby's unit came under some pretty heavy fire. Some sort of ambush, I gather. But your son acquitted himself real well. Fact is, he's up for a Silver Star."

"You're certain about this information," Riva said. "There's no chance for a mistake of some sort?"

"Well," Arlon said, "I don't think so, Riva. I'm very sorry."

The light in the room seemed to fade, to drain away like water escaping, blanched and wasting as we sat there. Arlon was talking, but his words arrived from a blanketed distance, distorted and incomprehensible. My ears rang and nausea surfaced and climbed in my legs, into my belly, and I stood abruptly; the room keeled and Arlon stood up with me, clearly alarmed, speaking to me, but I could not understand what he said. I made my way to the bathroom, dropped to my knees, vomited, stomach clenching and releasing, vomited again, my body peppered with sweat, working for breath as if I had run a long distance. I stood to brace myself against the wall and Riva was with me, pressing a towel to my face, her eyes filling with tears.

"He's alive, Sapper," she whispered into my ear. "He's alive."

Arlon's shape filled the hallway beyond the bathroom door. "You gonna be okay there, buddy?"

"I'll be all right," I said.

I held Riva a moment, then stepped past her, out of the bathroom, and turned to walk directly to the porch. Arlon joined me where I stood at the edge of the planking, looking east, toward the river.

"I needed some air," I said. We stood together a moment before I told Arlon how much I appreciated his help.

"Don't mention it. Least I could do. Just sorry it has to be this kind of news."

"Better than some other news you might've brought."

"I guess," Arlon said.

"When's he coming home?"

"That's a little unclear, but it won't be long. Maybe a couple weeks. I took the liberty of arranging his transfer to the VA hospital in Clarksburg. I hope that's what you and Riva want."

"He'll be nearby. That's good."

"Listen, Sapper, that was no joke about the Silver Star. Bob's commanding officer couldn't say enough about the boy. Seems he was first man out in this skirmish, took a hell of a personal risk. I gather he saved most of his own men and eliminated a bunch of the bad guys. Your son's a legitimate hero."

"Well," I said. "I'm not surprised."

Robins pecked in the front yard. A car passed along Delmartin Street, and Arlon said he needed to get back to the office.

"Thanks again," I said.

"Tell Riva goodbye for me."

"I will."

"And give Bobby my best. Tell him welcome home."

I nodded.

Arlon stood another moment before he stepped off the porch and walked quickly to his car.

I remained on the porch for some time after Arlon was gone. The springtime air shouldered a faithful simplicity I knew from all the seasons before, counting back to the beginnings of memory, effortless, transparent: so many seasons from this porch, this view of a street, the filtering treeline on the small bluff that fell away to the river. I smelled the heat approaching under the days, summer advancing with its ordinary certainty, the cycling rains and brilliant glaze of midday skies, curves of light rising and falling and rising again.

The door opened and Riva stepped onto the porch to join me.

"Arlon gone?"

"Some time ago," I said.

"I had to wait until he was gone."

"Yes," I said.

"Bobby's alive, Sapper. I thought we'd lost him. God forgive me for thinking that, but I did."

"Riva," I said, "I don't know what to think. I don't know *how* to think."

"He's alive," Riva said. "He's coming home. Nothing else matters now. We'll meet the rest as it comes."

"I didn't want him to go. I never wanted him to go."

"Don't get into that, Sapper. Don't do that to yourself."

"Riva . . ." I said, and could not continue.

"We have our son," she said. "That's what matters."

"Yes," I said. "Yes."

8

RIVA AND I stopped at a semicircular desk in the lobby of the Veterans Administration Hospital, where a woman flipped a series of soiled and brittle pages on a clipboard. *Here we are – Reeves, south wing, sixth floor. Room 612. Take Elevator B to six and turn right when you get off.*

We saw him from the doorway, his back turned toward us. He was standing at the window in hospital pajamas and bathrobe, a swath of furrowed bandages wrapped around his head. He had lifted the window several inches; a morning breeze cut across the overheated room. Then he heard us and turned and stood and we saw the bandage drawn across the right side of his face and his right arm dangling in a sling. His expression was tentative, peculiarly youthful, as if time had crossed in reverse in the months of his absence. He did not smile, or speak.

Riva burst into tears and stepped across the room to grasp him in both arms and she held him as he held her with his left arm, his face cradled on her shoulder. Oh God, Riva said against her crying, so good to see you, so wonderful to have you back. Then she let go to pull a tissue from her purse, and he came to me and I held him, feeling the bulk of his bandaged right arm propped between us, the acrid medicinal smell of ointments and linen bandages.

"Bobby," I said. "Welcome home."

"Dad," he said quietly. The sound of his voice startled me, its familiarity so absolute yet nearly forgotten. When he pulled back, he stepped around his bed and sat on the side facing the window.

I held to my spot in the middle of the room. Riva moved to where I stood and held my hand. "Everything okay in here?" she asked. "They're taking proper care of you?"

Bob spoke without turning around, saying it was certainly beautiful, this landscape, these trees. "I missed this place awful," he said. "Like you wouldn't believe."

"You hear things about these VA hospitals," Riva said. "I just want to know you're getting good care."

A moment clicked past before Bob said anything. "Good care? Yeah, I think so. I guess so. Not much to care for. I'm on the mend."

"That's good to hear," I said.

"Sure," Bob said. "On the mend. Right and proper."

We visited every day. Bob had trouble making eye contact but would sit in a chair to face us. His arm came out of the sling, and soon the bandage was a short wrap over his wrist. He graduated to a black eye patch and made uneasy conversation about idle matters: baseball scores, a television show he watched in the hospital dayroom, the prettiest nurse on the unit. I was happy for any sort of conversation at all.

The day before his release a psychiatrist intercepted Riva

and me in the corridor near the elevator, introduced himself as Dr. Kern, and asked us to join him in his office for a few minutes. We sat stiffly in Naugahyde chairs and the psychiatrist tapped a pencil against his desk blotter.

"I thought I should introduce myself, touch base with you folks, let you know what I think might be going on with your son."

"And what is that?" Riva said.

The psychiatrist flicked a glance toward her, saying he needed to let us know that veterans in Bob's situation were likely to have some significant readjustment problems.

"We don't expect it to be easy," I said. "How could it be?"

"Exactly," Kern said.

"What is it you wanted to tell us?" Riva asked.

"I've been talking to Bob the last few days, Mrs. Reeves, and he's probably doing about as well as we can expect. But mutilating injuries such as his can have very debilitating long-term effects. Not just the physical impairment. It's something we in psychiatry talk about called body image."

Kern paused, looking at us as if we might also be subjects for his professional consideration. Riva and I waited for him to continue.

"When an individual loses a part of his body," he said, "it can sometimes lead to an unconscious belief that he's not . . . well, not *complete*. I mean in the emotional sense. As if he lost some part of his . . ."

"Soul," I said.

Kern forced a short laugh. "That's probably a little too colorful a way to put it, but yes, that's close to what I'm trying to say."

"I don't think it's too colorful," I said. "It seems pretty accurate."

"Look," Kern said, "I'm simply saying that your son may need a good deal more help in coming to terms with what's happened to him. And we're here to do exactly that, to help. It wouldn't be a bad idea to set up a few appointments on an outpatient basis."

"Come to terms?" I said. My voice rose. "Why is it everybody's always trying to come to terms? Why don't we —"

Riva touched my knee to stop me and leaned forward. "We'll keep your offer in mind," she said.

Kern studied me, dispassionate. "Was there something you wanted to say, Mr. Reeves?"

"No," I said. "Nothing important."

Kern shrugged, lifted his chin, and pointed his pencil at the tray of business cards on the front edge of his desk. "Take one of my cards. Call anytime. Or have Bob call me, if he'd like."

"Thank you," Riva said, standing to go.

9

THE THREE of us side by side in my truck, Riva in the center, Bob at the window watching the countryside. A shower had moved through the valley at dawn and the smell of rain filled the patches of forest we traveled through. Greening foliage banked close to the roadside, the noon heat settling into the day. Bob kept his head turned to the window. For several miles he spoke only to answer our questions.

Well out of Clarksburg he turned to face forward and asked Riva about the produce market.

"It's going well," she said, relieved to be talking about something close and comfortable. "We've managed to grow since you spent your summers there."

"Grow?"

"As a business," Riva said. "Expand."

Bob offered a hard chuckle, the first sort of humor I had heard since his return. "Worked my ass off at that place." He glanced quickly toward Riva. "Excuse me," he said. "Worked my butt off."

Riva smiled. "Either way, it's true," she said. "But you always liked to work hard. You didn't want to sit around."

"That's true," he said.

"We're stocking local honey now from that hive over in Jarvisville," Riva continued. "It moves real well. Laura Kendall comes in two or three days a week and sells her vegetable soup from a little stand we put up in back. Miners headed to Farmington come by on the way to work and fill their Thermoses. Maybe pick up a bag of fruit for their wives."

Bob nodded slowly, as if he were constructing a picture in his mind of what had changed in the time he was away. "Kind of like to see the place," he murmured.

Riva looked at me. "We could go by. It's not too far out of the way. Sapper?"

"Sure," I said. "If that's what Bobby'd like to do."

"Never mind," Bob said quickly. "It was just a thought. It's not important."

"It's no problem," Riva said.

Bob looked out at the highway spinning toward us. "No," he said quietly. "Never mind."

10

ESTIN CAME from Memphis to visit. Bob smiled more easily for Estin than he did for us, accepted Estin's good-natured congratulations on a job well done, the random talk about being home where everyone belongs, having a lifetime ahead and plans to make. Riva roasted a turkey and we worked at a celebratory tone through the dinner.

It was over the apple pie that Estin said he'd never seen a genuine military combat decoration. He turned to Bob. "And you got the Silver Star! That's right up there close to the Medal of Honor, am I right?"

"Yes sir," Bob mumbled.

"Would you mind if I had a look?"

I sat back from the table, upright in my chair. Bob had not spoken about this medal, any of his medals. There were several: I had seen them, all except the Silver Star, on top of his dresser, piled together like trinkets carried home from a carnival.

"No," Bob said, "I guess I don't mind." He slipped away from the table.

Estin looked up at me, his expression mixing surprise and doubt. "Am I getting in a little too close here? We can let it go . . ."

"Let's move to the living room," Riva said. "I'll bring in some coffee."

Bob joined us, carrying a black velvet case and a leatherette binder with *United States Navy* embossed in gold on the cover. He handed them across to Estin. "They go together," he said. "They gave them to me before I left Nam. Some officer I'd never seen came to the hospital at Cam Ranh Bay, read the citation like he was late for lunch, and pinned the medal to my pajamas."

Riva stood, watching our son with a modulated caution. In the month since coming home, Bob had not placed this many words together at one time.

Estin looked up. "Bobby, if I'm out of line here, just say so. I don't mean to impose or be intrusive. Perhaps this isn't any of my business. Maybe we should save it for another time."

"Open the case," Bob said.

Estin did so: the medal rested against pale blue brocade, a tiny faceted star inset in the heart of a larger gold star, on a silk ribbon, blue and red stripes over a white background. Estin studied it and looked up again at Bob. "It's remarkable," he said. "I'm honored to be able to look at it."

Bob did not move from his position in the center of the room. Estin closed the case and placed it on an end table.

"You can read the citation," Bob said.

Estin looked down at the embossed lettering.

"Go ahead, read it."

Estin opened the binder. It was a single piece of paper, a typewritten paragraph with a smudged thumbprint on one margin, tucked under a transparent plastic sheet.

"Read it," Bob said.

"Listen, Bobby —"

"Go on and read it," Bob said. "Read it out loud."

Estin looked first at Riva, then at me, his eyes filled with apology. "Out loud?"

"That's right," Bob said. "We need to get this over with. You read it out loud and then everybody hears the story and I can put the damn thing away."

"Bobby —" Riva said.

"Go on, Estin," Bob said.

Estin reached his reading glasses from his shirt pocket and settled them low on the bridge of his nose and began to read, his voice filling the room *for conspicuous gallantry at the risk of his life above and beyond the call of duty while serving with Company B, 2nd Battalion, 5th Marines, in connection with combat operations against the enemy on the night of 21 April 1968. A small unit from Company B was on reconnaissance patrol when the unit came under a heavy volume of small arms and automatic weapons fire from a numerically superior enemy force occupying well-concealed emplacements in the surrounding jungle. The unit's ranking noncommissioned officer was killed instantly, as were two other Marines. During the ensuing fierce engagement, an enemy soldier managed to maneuver through the dense foliage to a position near the Marines, hurling a hand grenade which landed near Lance Corporal Reeves. Completely disregarding his personal safety, Lance Corporal Reeves picked up the grenade and threw it back into the enemy position, immediately disposing of three enemy sol-*

diers. Lance Corporal Reeves then rallied his comrades, moving forward into the fire-swept clearing to deliver withering machine gun fire into enemy ranks. Lance Corporal Reeves led a frontal assault that produced multiple enemy casualties, until he was severely wounded by a second hand grenade —

Estin's voice abruptly broke, and he stopped reading. He looked at each of us in turn.

"Go on," Bob said. "Finish it."

Estin drew a breath and looked back to the page. *Although in great pain, blinded in one eye, and weak from loss of blood, Lance Corporal Reeves continued to voice-direct fire, effectively resulting in full dispersal of the enemy. By his brilliant leadership, decisive action, and extraordinary courage, Lance Corporal Reeves reflected the highest credit upon himself and upheld the finest traditions of the Marine Corps and the United States Naval Service.*

Estin closed the portfolio and took off his reading glasses. Bob stood, motionless, staring into the center of the floor, his one eye stark and emptied.

11

ESTIN SWUNG his overnight bag into the trunk of his car.

"I feel bad around that business with Bobby," he told me. "He wasn't ready for that."

"No," I said, "I don't think he was."

"But Christ, that boy of yours did a job, didn't he? I can't help but think that same spirit will rescue him here before long. He'll save himself. He'll get past this bad time."

"I hope so."

Estin slammed the trunk closed, turned to lean against it. "I'm just sorry if I upset you all. You know I intended no harm."

"I know that, Estin. Anyway, things have to be faced sooner or later. You and I should know that, if anybody does."

"I guess so," he said. He crossed his arms across his chest. "We're still on for the Carnegie Hall show?"

I nodded. "Still on. Touch and go there for a while. Right after Bob came home, I wasn't too sure I gave a damn if I played there or anywhere else. If I ever played a note of music again." I looked toward the house. "But I think we have to do this show. The Still Creek Boys deserve this."

Estin grinned, the familiar affable smile, and he said, "I believe I agree with you on that point, old friend."

"Did you get in touch with Leonard? Tell him we're still on?"

"A small confession there, Sapper: I never called him to say otherwise."

I smiled.

"You know Leonard," Estin said. "It's not good to confuse him." He laughed, and asked if Riva and Bobby were coming up for the concert.

"Riva, of course," I said. "I'll have to talk to Bob."

We settled arrangements to pick up Leonard at the airport in Pittsburgh and spend a week of rehearsal in Maxwell before the trip to New York, and Estin was gone, down Delmartin Street before he turned right on Davis.

12

SITTING WITH Bob on the back porch.

We had carried out sandwiches with glasses of iced tea. Bob wore a cuffed bandage over the stump of his right hand. He balanced the sandwich on the stump's leveled surface between bites. I looked away.

Bob ate and gazed out to the yard and gave a cynical snort. "I used to play soldier," he said. "Right here in this yard."

"I remember. Those games got pretty wild sometimes."

"And everybody survived."

"No question about that."

"Funny thing, isn't it?" Bob said. "How common a game that was. How much fun we had playing it." He took another bite of his sandwich.

"You had a chance to call any of your friends since you've been back?"

Bob had been home nearly ten weeks, sleeping until midday, listening to the radio in his room, staring at the television into the small hours of the night. I knew he had called nobody but asked the question anyway.

"I'll get around to it," he said. "Most everybody's probably gone."

"I still see folks," I said. "Monty Wellman comes in the store pretty often. He asks about you."

"Yeah," Bob said, his voice flat. "Good old Monty."

We ate for a few minutes in silence, and I asked Bob if he would like to come to New York for the Carnegie Hall concert.

"That's all right," he said. "I'll be fine here. I'll keep the home fires burning."

"The home fires will be fine without you. And I think the trip would be good for you. Get the hell out of here. Hear some music. There'll be a lot of people up there in New York. It's a big show. I'd love to have you there."

"That's okay, Dad. I was never much of a country music fan anyway."

"It's just to get away, Bob. A different horizon."

"A different horizon. I hope I never have to see another different horizon in my life. I'm going to stay right here."

My irritation flickered, no different from when Bob was younger, headstrong and resistant. "You know," I said, "you're going to have to do more than sit here and let time slide by."

"Really?" Bob's voice was caustic.

"What're you going to do, sit in your room and grow old?"

"Sounds like a pretty good idea, if you ask me."

I lifted my iced tea for a sip, attempting to marshal a useful response.

"I mean, here we are," Bob said, maintaining the blade in

his voice, "and what could be better than this? Sitting on our back porch. Which is where I just might spend the rest of my life. So what?"

"Bob, I —"

"Just don't lean, Dad. Is that a possibility? About half my life I didn't see you more than two days a week, now you're going to . . . what, *hover?* I don't think so. I need a little air here."

"You've got all the air you need."

"Do I? Is that a fact? Truth is, I feel a little short of breath right about now."

"Bobby, you're being cruel. I'm simply trying to offer . . . some assistance."

"I'm fine. I'm *fine.* How many times do you need to hear that?"

"Bobby, you're not fine. This conversation is not fine. And it's okay to struggle. It's okay."

Bob glared straight ahead in a grimace, baring his teeth, a florid hate congealing in his face. He seemed to be no one I knew, had ever known.

"Son, your mother and I want to try and help you —"

"Help me? You want to *help* me? What the hell can you do to help me?" Bob abruptly took his plate in his left hand and flung it into the yard, spiraling china and bread and meat, cheese and wisps of lettuce flailing into the grass, his anger fountaining. He stood to look down at me, roaring, *"Look at me! I don't have a hand!"*

He picked up his iced tea, hurled the glass into a pillar. Tea and ice and shattered glass sprayed the porch's board flooring, and Bob ripped his eye patch away, snapping the rubber band and whirling to punch his face within a foot of mine.

"How about this?" His eyelid sucked into the empty

socket where the right eye had been, the skin of his temple and bridge of his nose puckered and bleached and pellet-scarred, his face in front of mine, afloat, about to speak — trying to speak — when he burst into violent tears and rocked past me, slamming into the house, leaving me rigid in the chair except for my quivering hands.

I sat with the abrupt silence of a summer day, floor at my feet slick with broken glass and ice, the bright grass beyond littered with the odd remains of a sandwich, the faceless white oval of an overturned plate.

The day's heat ascended and I sat, sundered, voiceless, alone.

13

I STOOD in front of Bob's bedroom door, hesitating before I tapped, lightly, three times. No response. There was the muffled sighing of his rage and sadness through the wood, the close hallway in half-light around me.

Darkness is always unexpected — never the plan one makes or attempts to imagine, every notion of control, of purpose or direction or ambition lost in the hard weather of the unforeseen, the feral accidents of time. The fresh summer day Bob and I had sat in minutes earlier was bright and new and I was exhausted simply by its prospect, the threat of so many hours left to live through.

"Bobby?" My voice dry, nearly a whisper.

No response.

Two more taps at the door.

Movement inside: a rustle, a footstep. The door swung wide and Bob stood. He looked oddly naked without his black eye patch.

"Bobby," I said, "I'm sorry."

His pallid face held in abeyance, rigid and distanced and empty.

"You're right about me pushing too hard. Things take the time they take."

Bob looked away from me. He was making a show of waiting. Let the old man say his piece and get the door closed again.

"Maybe it's hard to understand —"

"Maybe it is," he interrupted.

I paused and then continued. "Hard to understand my feelings, the feelings of a father, a parent. Somebody who's loved you all your life. Without reservation. Maybe these are feelings you have to be a father to understand." The words rang weak and repetitive but I let them stand. Bob did not speak.

"So it's hard not to want . . ." The current of my thought lost bearing and I drifted, a biting surge of grief pouring through the closed spaces of my mind.

"Not to want what?" Bob said.

"Well," I said. "To . . . help you."

I saw Bob swallow. "Okay," he said. "Good. I wish you luck."

"How about we go back out to the porch? Try this one more time."

"No thanks."

"Maybe take a walk?"

"I'm fine right here."

I allowed a few seconds to pass and then said, "I'll try not to hover, Bobby." I forced a smile.

"Dad," Bob said, "I'm just under" — he lifted his left hand, a grasping gesture — "a lot of pressure right now. I'm feeling a lot of pressure."

"I think I can understand that."

Bob offered a slight nod. "I mean," he said, very quietly, "I'm not too sure of anything right now."

We did not speak then, and in that abandoned minute between us we seemed nothing more than casualties of love and random circumstance, sad and isolated men on the hinge of a vacant world.

After a time I said, "If it means anything to you, I know that feeling all too well. A man can get there from all sorts of starting points."

Bob looked at me again, then stepped back in the doorway. "I'm tired," he said. "I need to lie down."

"Maybe we can take that walk a little later."

Bob only nodded, and swung his door slowly closed.

I heard the truck's engine and then Riva's brisk step across the porch, the parched crackle of grocery sacks hitting the kitchen table. I stood a moment longer in front of Bob's closed door.

In the kitchen I emptied bags, shelved the canned soup, put the milk and table cream and butter in the refrigerator.

"What is it?" Riva said.

"Bobby."

She stopped what she was doing, looking at me, waiting.

"He's all right, he's in his room. We were talking on the back porch."

"It didn't go so well, I gather."

"I asked him to come with us to New York for the concert."

"He didn't want to come?"

"No," I said, "he doesn't."

"I'm not really surprised. Were you?"

"I suppose I hadn't thought about it. It's not that, anyway. I got around to talking about *him,* what he's doing — sitting around here like a zombie."

Riva studied me. "You used different words from those, I hope."

"I was gentler than that, but I guess I still came at him too hard. He lost his temper . . ."

"And?"

I sat in one of the chairs at the table. "So what do we do? Let him sit?"

Riva turned back to the groceries, emptied the last bag, and folded it away beneath the sink. "You think we should get him down to the VA hospital to see that doctor?"

"I don't know. Would it matter? Would he go?" I looked through the window, into the neighbor's sycamore. "All we wanted," I said, "was to have him back. To have him alive and home. The single and most desperate desire. We never gave a moment's thought to how he would come back. To who he would be when he came back."

"Nobody thinks like that, Sapper. Nobody imagines terrible things happening to their child. Nobody *should.*"

"No," I said, "you're right, of course. And now we thank the angels he's here, sitting in his room, and take the rest of it a day at a time?"

"It's the only way open to us. It's all we can do." Riva moved to stand behind me and gripped my shoulders, then leaned down to embrace me, her mouth at my ear, and she said again, "It's all we can do."

14

PLAYING WITH the Still Creek Boys in a tavern near Enterprise, West Virginia, a Saturday night in the early summer of 1954. Estin and Leonard packed in a shadowed corner behind me as I played the last song of the night, looking out across the heads of the patrons still remaining to hear my voice resonate in the cinder-block square of that plain little building, and it seems as if I knew as much then as I do now, design and pattern shimmering along the years and the unfathomed distance below, the collaborations of time returning always to the common heart.

I finished and waved an appreciation toward the scatter of handclaps, dropped down from the stage and cased my instrument, and rose to see Riva standing near the open door, next to the bar. The glow of the lamps sculpted her face and glossed her hair. She smiled and I walked to her, seeing our truck through the door, parked squarely in front.

Is everything all right?

Everything's fine, Riva said. Just fine.

What're you doing out here? At this hour?

It seems your son couldn't sleep. He padded out in his pajamas and asked where his daddy was. I told him you were working, playing music. He asked if you were very far away and I said not too far, so he asked if I'd bring him out to hear you play. But he just couldn't keep his eyes open once we got on the road.

Bobby's in the truck?

Sound asleep.

What about you? I asked. Did you get to hear any music?

Three songs, yes. And they were beautiful. Especially that last one.

I looked out into the night, toward the truck.

Let me take the two of you home, I said.

Interstate 79 North, West Virginia, June 16, 1997

The Stonewall Jackson Reservoir rises to my right, the water black and featureless as sunrise edges the hills. Hours beyond Nashville, and Kentucky behind me.

The hunched seam of the mountains follows to the west, the sky past haunting in this first flare of arriving day, and I consider my life in its passage, lived and recalled and still deep in its voyage. I can ask what history offers that cannot be seen for simply looking, but it is more than this, a sheltered message like an unexpected meadow one might come upon deep in a forest, a secret light in the everyday world that, in the end, must be earned and loved and constantly rediscovered.

In another hour I will go through the door on Delmartin Street, take off my shoes, and slip out of my clothes to lie beside Riva. She will still be asleep in our bed, warm and turned into the soft and falling light, and will wake next to me, and I will be home once again, knowing that a man and a woman search for each other through all the years they are together even as they fail to understand the bristling surges and abandoned moments and antagonistic possibilities that any love encompasses. I have always wanted Riva, loved her, desired her, the certainty in that knowledge a justification that never left me but did little to save me, that often served only to recall my frailties of character. If Riva stood always against the corrosive energy of my despair, it was surely the only position she could take. She was correct in this as she has been correct in so many things, a woman of pure and unstinting intuition with a refined ability to assess her own heart even as it turned from me.

One learns with time to recite litanies of misdirection with far less compunction, while still offering a raised hand of sanction and acknowledgment to the scattered flares of regret that remain, one's very own for the keeping. A man shears away the latticework of his life to look squarely into the river of his days, stranded there by a moment of profound recognition as he understands the precise and contradictory nature of his salvation, as every morning still comes in search of what he believes, still asking by what measure he will stand up and move.

Bob is as old now as I was when he returned from Vietnam, our lives so different as to be nearly inconceivable that we are father and son. He has never married, lives alone in an apartment, teaches civics and history at the high school. For years he seemed to live on a winter coastline, staring out at the metallic sea of his mind, waiting, I supposed, waiting and working along the edges of his isolation's forced dignity. I remained as close to him as I could, as close as he would permit, moving against the grain, offering an array of recommendations, suggestions, entreaties, pleas, feeling all the while the barren miles inside my words. Anguish became a greed of its own intent and direction, feeding between us on nothing more than the sand at our feet as I squatted between fear and hope, my guilt at events I could never have controlled or stopped returning with unassailable frequency.

When Bob lurched away from what happened to him it did not come as revelation: no cardinal moment of ardent self-apprehension, no redemptive blaze. I knew his private fire continued to jitter like heat lightning in some silent and resistant distance as he began to frame a life, a place to live in the world, a daily round he could accept. These days he volunteers one day a week at the VA hospital, working with other disabled veterans. He has listened to veterans of Panama and Lebanon and the Gulf War, and when he speaks of this work, or himself — which is still rarely — it is in modest tones, his own quiet surprise in how time has made him the listener, the one who now insists on the validity of life with all its unexpected travesties.

Once he asked me to pick him up at the hospital when his car was in for repair, and I was directed from the front desk to a ward on the hospital's east side. I stepped out of the elevator and walked down the corridor, glancing into the rooms, and I saw Bob where a door stood partially opened. He was sitting at a bedside and watching the man in the bed with an intensity I remembered in striking echo from his boyhood — the clarity and natural force in the angle of his face, his inspiriting fearlessness. I waited there a moment in the corridor. The man in the bed said something — his head was turned away from me — and Bob said, It feels that way now. But it won't feel that way forever. Trust me on this point. *The man in the bed lifted his hand and Bob took it and they held their hands clasped together and Bob said,* Nothing changes, but how you feel about that and what you make of it is always up to you. *I was startled by the careful urgency in his prescience, feeling a pained contrition as I stood in the corridor's watery daylight. Bob looked up, waved, and stood to put on his coat. He exchanged a few more words with the man in the bed and walked out to join me.*

We reached the elevator and stood together, waiting, and I said, This is good work that you do.

Bob looked at me, smiled, and touched my arm.

I played in Alan Bernstein's concert at Carnegie Hall with a reunited Still Creek Boys, and we have since played there two more times. I have recorded five albums in the past decade; young and well-known musicians join me now in the studio, eager to appear. Journalists travel to Maxwell once or twice a year to create and maintain generous fictions about my life, none of them realizing that I do not know and have never known where music comes from, or why. I never truly believed that music, mine or anyone else's, might change anything so impenetrable as the way we live, our human limitations and mad insistence on defeat and sorrow, but I have trusted always that a song bears its own justice into the world. Music is among the few things we possess with any kind of innate spirit and private knowledge, an honest embrace of its own, a welcome heat that arrives of its own accord and when least expected from some proud and mysterious heaven.

And when the journalists ask where my songs come from,

I tell them about the summer I was eighteen years old, standing under a willow tree beside Redroe Creek on Waterhill Ridge, looking up into the tree's long-tendril leaves. The wind moved slightly in the boughs, and the sky above the tree was cloudless, a blue of such intensity and depth it was nearly iridescent. Standing there, looking up, I began to sing to myself, wordlessly, an arrangement of notes, the beginning of a melody. After dinner I took my banjo outside, sat on the edge of the porch, and began to play. The melody I carried through that day became the song "Miranda," although I had never met a woman named Miranda, nor is there any mention in the song of a willow tree or a visionary sky or a narrow creek on the side of a lost mountain, but those are the roots of a song I have played all my life, thousands of times, in hundreds of places.

Most of my songs originated in the same random and inexplicable way. I carried them all out on the road with the band, writing more as we traveled, fragments and edges of words or music or both, small legends of the miles. I watched the land bend and rise and fall, the big empty days filled with mountains and clouds and the cold black shine of the sculpted nights as we drove on to another town and another show, dead leaves slicing and whirling to paste flat against the Chrysler's misted windows. One night we passed a farmboy in bib overalls sitting astride a milk cow and waiting to cross the two-lane. He watched us come and go and I saw myself in that boy, no different from the boy I once was, waiting and looking into the unknown future as if it might reveal its design out of the shapeless dreams of the earth.

Route 19 flattens into the valley of the river I have lived beside for most of my life. The sky is a wisping mix of frail color, iris pinks and shredded haze, the empty highway bearing me into town. I remember the boy on the cow alongside the road as I turned to see a rush of leaves whipping and blowing back from the wet tires, away down the glistening highway as the boy disappeared inside the night, all that backwoods wonder awash. I turn off Main and float the truck down to Delmartin, turn north again, and come to a stop in front of my house, hearing drifting remnants of music played years before and miles away, indelible and still alive somewhere in the fields of the world, in the mountain rain, in the opening light.